©lack

GOBLIN SLAYER
SIDE STORY II

DAI KATANA

The Singing Death 3

©lack

PRAY AND PLAY,

ADVENTURER!

"A shame,
a great shame.
But I'm afraid
your adventure
ends here."

The red blade is
the symbol of death.
You, and your cousin,
all your companions,
are going to die.
There will be no
exceptions. Not one.
For no one can escape
the Death.

©lack

# CONTENTS

Step VI
DEAD SPACE
.
.
003

Step VII
LAIR OF THE EVIL SAMURAI
.
.
081

Step VIII
DAI KATANA: THE SINGING DEATH
.
.
101

Step IX
YOUTH AND ASHES, SIDE BY SIDE
.
.
129

DAI KATANA

The Singing Death

# GOBLIN SLAYER

## SIDE STORY II

### The Singing Death

## KUMO KAGYU

ILLUSTRATION BY lack

YEN ON
New York

# GOBLIN SLAYER
## SIDE STORY II
# DAI KATANA
The Singing Death

KUMO KAGYU ③ ILLUSTRATION BY lack

Translation by Kevin Steinbach ✦ Cover art by lack

This book is a work of fiction. Names, characters, places, and incidents are the product of the author's imagination or are used fictitiously. Any resemblance to actual events, locales, or persons, living or dead, is coincidental.

GOBLIN SLAYER GAIDEN 2: DAI KATANA GE
Copyright © 2022 Kumo Kagyu
Illustrations copyright © 2022 lack
All rights reserved.
Original Japanese edition published in 2022 by SB Creative Corp.
This English edition is published by arrangement with SB Creative Corp., Tokyo in care of Tuttle-Mori Agency, Inc., Tokyo.

English translation © 2024 by Yen Press, LLC

Yen On
150 West 30th Street, 19th Floor, New York, NY 10001

Visit us at yenpress.com • facebook.com/yenpress • twitter.com/yenpress
yenpress.tumblr.com • instagram.com/yenpress

First Yen On Edition: January 2024
Edited by Yen On Editorial: Rachel Mimms
Designed by Yen Press Design: Wendy Chan

Yen On is an imprint of Yen Press, LLC.
The Yen On name and logo are trademarks of Yen Press, LLC.

The publisher is not responsible for websites (or their content) that are not owned by the publisher.

Library of Congress Cataloging-in-Publication Data
Names: Kagyū, Kumo, author. | lack (Illustrator), illustrator.
Title: Goblin Slayer side story II: dai katana / Kumo Kagyu ; illustration by lack.
Other titles: Goblin Slayer gaiden 2: tsubanari no daikatana. English
Description: First Yen On edition. | New York : Yen On, 2020–
Identifiers: LCCN 2020043585 | ISBN 9781975318239 (v. 1 ; trade paperback) |
ISBN 9781975333539 (v. 2 ; trade paperback) | ISBN 9781975376994 (v. 3 ; trade paperback)
Subjects: LCSH: Goblins—Fiction. | GSAFD: Fantasy fiction.
Classification: LCC PL872.5.A367 G5313 2020 | DDC 895.63/6—dc23
LC record available at https://lccn.loc.gov/2020043585

ISBNs: 978-1-9753-7699-4 (paperback)
978-1-9753-7700-7 (ebook)

10 9 8 7 6 5 4 3 2 1

LSC-C

Printed in the United States of America

# GOBLIN SLAYER
### SIDE STORY II
# DAI KATANA
#### The Singing Death

3

# Characters

You Are the Hero

## YOU

### G-SAM
### HUMAN MALE

At the entrance to the Dungeon of the Dead in the northern reaches of the Four-Cornered World, there is a fortress city. A human adventurer has just arrived there. He is a warrior who has mastered the ways of the sword.

Blessed
Hardwood Spear

## FEMALE WARRIOR

### N-FIG
### HUMAN FEMALE

A girl you meet in the fortress city. An "old hand," she's already been down in the dungeon. A human warrior who wields a spear.

Sword Maiden Lily

## FEMALE BISHOP

### G-BIS
### HUMAN FEMALE

A girl you meet at the tavern in the fortress city. She lost her eyes on a previous adventure. She can identify items by the power of the Supreme God.

# DAIKATANA | The Singing Death

One of the All-Stars

## COUSIN
## G-MAG
## HUMAN  FEMALE

Your older cousin, who accompanied you to the fortress city. She's a kind woman who looks after you like a sister would, but sometimes you think she's not all there. A human wizard, she supports you from the back row.

Hawkwind

## HALF-ELF SCOUT
## N-THI
## HALF ELF  MALE

An adventurer you met on your way to the fortress city. As entertaining as he is keen-eyed, he serves as your party's scout.

Elite Solar Trooper, Special Agent, and Four-Armed Humanoid Warrior Ant

## MYRMIDON MONK
## G-PRI
## MYRMIDON  MALE

An adventurer you met in the fortress city. An old hand in the dungeon, he serves as your party's strategist. He is a Myrmidon or "Bugman Monk" who serves the Trade God.

©lack

Those who knew how it began were no more.

Perhaps some unfortunate farmer moved a stone that should have stayed put. Maybe some foolish child undid a seal in a shrine somewhere. It may have even been a fiery stone shooting across the heavens.

Whatever the cause, it was not so very long ago that the Death began stalking the continent.

Disease traveled on the wind, consuming all the people it encountered; the dead rose, the trees withered, the air grew foul and the water rancid.

The King of Time issued a proclamation: "Find the source of this Death and seal it away."

Thus heroes arose all over the continent, and so they, too, were swallowed one by one by the Death, leaving nothing but their corpses.

The only exception was a single party, which left these words alone:

"The maw of the Death lies in the northernmost reaches."

None left knew who discovered this. For those adventurers, too, were spirited away by the Death.

The Dungeon of the Dead.

The entrance to this vast abyss yawned like the jaws of the Reaper, and people gathered at the foot of it, until finally a fortress city was born.

In this city, adventurers sought companions, challenged the dungeon, battled, found loot…and sometimes died.

These days of glory went on, and on, and on, repeating over and over.

Riches and monsters welled up without end—as did the incessant hack and slash.

Life was spilled like so much water as adventurers drowned in their own dreams until the fire disappeared from their eyes.

Sooner or later, all that remained, glowing like an ember, were the ashen days of adventuring, which went hand in hand with the Death…

*The man in black disappears into the darkness, and you and your companions chase after him.*

How simple it would be if that was how the story went. Instead, however, your party is left standing in the chamber, battered, beaten, and defeated. You're all ragged. No one even tries to speak. The faint weeping you hear—is that Female Bishop? Is that Female Warrior's anguished moan?

It was a struggle of life and death, and you've emerged on the other side. You've triumphed and survived, overcome the trials, and earned the right to go beyond them.

The inky abyss yawns before you. A labyrinth of magic and murder calls to you—the Dungeon of the Dead.

But why would you go there?

It's all too clear what waits beyond. Not the man in black—the thing that lurks behind him.

The Death.

Small piles of ash remain in the chamber—piles of ash that used to be people, used to be adventurers before they burned until they were nothing but cinders.

You breathe in some of the ash, then breathe out again. Even breathing seems repugnant to you, but if you don't do it, it will all end here.

Hence why no one, none of you, makes a move—nor even thinks of moving.

You stand stock still, your breath escaping you like a groan. You realize you're still clutching your katana. Your fingers are stiff as stone and shaking. They seem frozen to the hilt, and you can't get them to let go of your own accord.

Three times: You take deliberate deep breaths, let them out again, and finally your fingers begin to loosen.

You flick the blood off your blade—the weapon shines as if it hasn't cut anything at all—and then return it to its scabbard.

Only then, at last, do you speak to the others. You tell them it's time to go.

"G-go…?" Female Warrior stammers, as if she doesn't understand the meaning of the word.

You nod. You have to go. Standing here will gain no one anything. You'll head back up top, regroup, and lick your wounds. If you aren't going to move forward, then that is the only other possibility open to you.

"…"

However, your cousin—always the first to get behind an idea—is silent. She stares down into the abyss with her probing, perceptive gaze. Her slim fingers reach toward her mouth.

"Fusion Blast didn't work? Did I do something wrong? Was that the Dungeon Master? Impossible. And yet…"

She chews on her thumbnail and mumbles to herself, a mage grappling with the truth. Hers is the face of a spell caster in an accomplished party who understands that if she doesn't transcend her own spells, everyone will die.

A moment later, though, the look is gone; she sees you watching her and grins at you—now this is the face of your *second* cousin. "Yeah, that's right!" she says with the relentless cheerfulness you've come to expect of her. Her voice booms in the silent chamber. She thrusts an arm in the air hard enough to disperse the miasma in the dungeon all by herself. "We've found the way forward. We can't shrink back now!"

"Right…" Female Bishop reaches under the bandage over her eyes, rubbing her eyelids as she stands up. The blue ribbon her friend left to her is tied firmly around an arm otherwise covered in ash. She grips the sword and scales and nods decisively. "Whatever else, we must destroy that thing. If we aren't in top shape when we challenge it, we'll never win." Her voice is shaking, yet strong. Strong enough to make your eyes widen.

"If that's the plan," Half-Elf Scout says with a chuckle, "we'll need a war chest."

You ask if he trusts he can do it, to which he nods and replies, "Yeah, sure. At the very least, I can start by rifling through a treasure chest. Gimme a minute?"

Then comes the clacking of mandibles: "...I don't really care either way."

Half-Elf Scout responds to Myrmidon Monk's declaration with a guffaw. "Life or death, and you ain't got a preference?"

Everyone is pushing hard to create this relaxed atmosphere—and you're grateful. Female Bishop and Myrmidon Monk put their heads together over the map, plotting a route home. Half-Elf Scout heads for the locked treasure chest as your cousin trots beside him declaring, "I'll help!"

Everyone is busy fulfilling their own roles.

So you, for your part, walk over to Female Warrior, who's crouched down and looking shattered.

"...!"

She sucks in a breath when she hears your footsteps; her shoulders give one great shake, and she shrinks even further into herself. The spear in her hand is broken, ruined; it will never serve in combat again. Yet Female Warrior hugs the shaft and refuses to let go. She isn't like Female Bishop, clasping what she has lost close to her heart. Instead, she clings to the spear because it is her only haven; because if she lets it go, she fears she will disappear.

And what can *you* say to a girl who feels like that?

There is only one thing you can do: stay silent and stand beside her, as you always do. Amidst the susurrus of shifting ash as the others move around, you can just catch the girl's faint moans.

Time is a slippery thing down in the dungeon. How long has passed since that life-and-death struggle? A day? A few hours? Or mere minutes?

You resolve to simply stand and wait—suddenly you feel a gentle weight, and a warmth, against your leg. Female Warrior has come close and pressed her face to you. "The older girls," she manages. "They all… They all died…"

The whisper falls from her lips, and it seems to unveil the well-spring of the will that has brought her this far. She believed that in the depths of the Death, there might be life. But it was not so. There is Death, and Death alone.

But that is enough to make one think, *Perhaps it is time to stop.* However wrung out one may be, as long as one has a goal, one can take the next step, no matter how unsteady. Yet once one arrives, how is one to take the step after that? Especially when one has used up every ounce of one's strength—and found nothing.

Perhaps it's not possible to go on believing forever that bliss is always just on the other side of the mountain. And yet in your mind, that's better than those who jeer and say that there is no bliss at all in the world.

To find out, she got to her feet, walked, and came this far: five floors down, into the heart of the Dungeon of the Dead, farther than anyone had gone before. It would be beyond the hack-and-slashers with their cute little maps.

Only an adventurer could do what she has done.

You have no words to say to a young woman who lost her family, her friends, all at a stroke. But to a young woman who risked everything to take the next step and try to save those family and friends—to her, there is something you can say.

You reach out a gauntleted hand and brush Female Warrior's head as gently as the falling snow. It's not a gesture of comfort but of praise for a job well done.

"……*Hic*… Ohhh…!"

She sniffles, then snorts, then cries, the sounds evading her attempts to stifle them. You simply continue stroking her hair, so black it seems to vanish against the darkness of the chamber.

It's as simple as this:

When you were about to die, when the spark within you guttered…

Indeed, even from the first moment you resolved to challenge this dungeon…

Has she not been with you, walking by your side? Shoulder to shoulder with all your companions?

Yes. This is not your story alone.

Female Bishop, your cousin, Myrmidon Monk, and Half-Elf Scout have all gotten help from her at times you don't even know about.

In which case, how could you ever resent waiting for her to stand up?

Shortly thereafter, the weeping turns to a quiet sniffle, and you judge that it is time. You ask softly if she can make it to the top, not if she can go back. Whether you return to confront the dungeon depths or choose to stop here, you will be moving forward.

Female Warrior looks at you vacantly, her eyes as damp and as clear as a lake at twilight, deep enough to swallow you whole.

At length, she says, "Yeah…," in the voice of a little girl tired from crying. Her slim, delicate hand reaches out and brushes your fingers, then entwines itself with them. You squeeze back, then help heft her to her feet.

Female Warrior rises slowly, languorously, like she's stretching; the heels of her sabbatons click on the floor.

"Looks like this spear is done for," she says. "Guess I'll be counting on you until we reach the top." She gives you that catlike smile and laughs with a sound like a tinkling bell. Then she smacks you on the shoulder and turns around.

You nod to her back, tell her you'll take care of things. Be they slimes, goblins, or bushwhackers, let them come. Let them try you if they dare.

*I will cut them down, every single one.*

§

Along with a rustle of wind, the first thing you notice is the smell of the country burning.

It's supposed to be nighttime, but it's bright—and not because the fortress city never sleeps.

You can see the twinkling of flames in the distance, sending up thick smoke that blots out the light of the twin moons and the stars.

From the dungeon on the edge of town, you have an excellent view. From beyond the city walls, something flows like a black river toward the city, reaching out from endlessly far away toward the town.

It's people—the squirming shapes heading for the city, civilians and defeated soldiers. Survivors, somehow, of hexes overpowered and overwhelmed, they've come to the northmost reaches in search of some kind of hope.

It's the feeling of an ending. You think you can taste cold ash that no longer harbors even the last lingering warmth of any fire.

The Four-Cornered World has been scorched and singed.

"...The heck's goin' on?" Half-Elf Scout asks, stunned. Unable to even put on a merry expression, he focuses his sharp eyes (a bequest of one of his parents) and looks into the distance, then lets out a low groan.

"Do you think...a war's broken out?" Female Bishop asks, raising her chin slightly and sniffing the air. Her tone is solemn, and she barely squeezes out the end of her question. Not from fear, but from caution; a vigilant search for the enemy's true form. In spite of the awful things she's experienced, Female Bishop's face is taut as a bowstring. The Death in the air must be all the more detectable to her, deprived of her sight.

"If so, it's been raging for a long time," Myrmidon Monk says with clacking mandibles. The antennae on his forehead shake, and then in a tone that suggests he wants to cut down all the stupid humans, he continues, "This was the front line—not that anybody here acted like they cared."

You don't even see any sign of the royal guards who normally stand watch here. Not just the woman you're used to seeing—there isn't a single soldier anywhere. Yet you don't feel you can say that this is a lack of vigilance.

There's simply something more important happening.

Although it's a fact that, at this moment, you can't imagine what would be more pressing than the Dungeon of the Dead.

"Let's hurry!" your cousin says, without even looking at you. "If we need information, the tavern is the place to go!"

*Ah, there it is.* You give Female Warrior a gentle pat on the back, and then you run like the wind.

You're exhausted. All you want to do is fall into bed and sleep like a log, but your eyes are clear, your mind working. Half-Elf Scout catches up and overtakes you, and Myrmidon Monk is close behind him. Lastly, Female Bishop says, "Let's go!" and Female Warrior nods and says, "Right."

Then you hear three sets of hurrying footsteps. Fine, then. If your cousin is with them, that's fine.

What's not fine is the scene in town.

"They're *all* refugees…!" Half-Elf Scout says, and you understand his amazement.

The town you knew is gone—the fortress city had belonged to the adventurers who walked the streets as if they owned the place, but now there's no trace of that. The streets are packed instead with crowds of people in ragged, scruffy clothing.

Strangely, no one appears to have any baggage to speak of. And though there are many tired faces, no one seems panicked.

These, you realize, are the ones who were smart enough to abandon everything and flee with only the clothes on their backs in order to save themselves. That was why they got into the fortress city first. Those less canny are the source of that great black river out there.

You know, too, that the Death will gradually approach and dry that river up.

*It's a strange thing.* You realize your mouth has softened into a smile without your noticing it. How strange, that although the Death emanates from that dungeon, this fortress city should be the last place to succumb to it.

You open the door of the Golden Knight and walk into a bustle of an entirely different kind from usual.

"Somebody help! There were demons hiding in the village! Disguised as children… They killed everyone!"

"A dragon! We were attacked by a dragon! The sky burned! The tower crumbled in an instant…!"

"My village was destroyed by goblins… Somebody…somebody help me!"

"Goblins can wait, dumbass! All that shit can wait! The undead are coming, and I want everyone who can hold a weapon to help me face them down!"

"They came back… They were dead, and then…they started getting up! All of them, shambling to their feet…"

Some yell, some tremble with fear, some beg, some argue, and some simply curl into themselves, muttering. The Golden Knight is no longer a place for adventurers' meetings and partings. Everyone shouts and cries, makes a case for their own tragedy.

Not because they expect anyone to save them. No, not at all. They don't even care if someone, anyone, hears them. They simply need to let the emotions out.

For one thing, there's no Adventurers Guild in the fortress city. Rank tags mean nothing here. If you want to beg help from an adventurer, the tavern is the only place to go—and most of the city's adventurers there at that moment appear to regard the uproar as nothing but a nuisance.

You still can't shake that sense of ash as you call out to a familiar waitress.

"Yes? I'm sorry," she starts and then says "I mean, welcome back!" She hurries up to you, her rabbit ears—yes, they are real—bobbing as she goes. She greets you with gladness for your safety, but then the small talk is over and she gives you an apologetic look. "You see how it is—we don't have a single open table today."

Now that she mentions it, you notice that the round table where your party always sits is already occupied by some refugees. So much for gathering intelligence—at this rate, you won't even be able to sit down and take a break.

You flip the waitress a gold coin, asking if she wouldn't be able to bring some food and drinks for several people, and quickly.

"Sure thing! Coming right up!" the rabbit-eared server says, tucking the coin into the cleft of her chest and rushing back to the kitchen.

"This looks like it could be a very big problem," your cousin says, gazing around. You offer a brief word of agreement.

*In fact…*

This has been, to borrow Myrmidon Monk's phrase, a big problem that's been raging for a long time. The destruction of this world began long ago; you and yours simply weren't willing to face it. It's only now that many people realize how close the Death has pressed upon the world.

"So what do we do?" your cousin asks. How strange. What is there to question or hesitate about now?

You answer. *First...*

"First?" she says.

First, you go back to the inn and rest.

You state it as a fact. The situation is clear, and what you must do is equally clear. You've endured a life-or-death struggle in the dungeon and have returned to the surface. You need to recuperate, identify what you got in your haul, and then go from there.

Your cousin blinks at the total conviction in your words, but then her face softens ever so slightly. "Yes, you're exactly right!" As she smiles like a blossoming flower, you sigh in relief. This is one thing you've always admired about your *second* cousin.

The server returns and you take your dinner from her, then trail out of the tavern with your companions in tow. Each of them says whatever's on their mind, and naturally, conversation develops. Throughout, though, Female Warrior offers not a word, only noncommittal grunts and nods. But that's understandable.

As you walk through the fortress city, now veritably turned upside down by the influx of refugees, you look up at the sky. It's as bright as the town—not only the stars, but even the smoke rising from the distant mountain are invisible.

*So what?*

That's right—no reason to get upset. Flailing around would do no one any good this late in the game.

The beginning of the end: That's all this is.

*We're approaching the climax.*

§

Whatsoever happens to the squares, the sun will rise upon the board.

Bright beams of light cascade down out of a pale blue sky, and you sit up on your mound of straw.

Thankfully, there was still space in the stables and the economy room—a lucky turn of the pips. When you think of all those who have lost their homes, their lodgings, and had to sleep on the dusty roadside...

You murmur to yourself as you brush some straw off your chin that it's a curious thing. You don't think you did well, or were uncommonly skillful, or even that you took anything from anyone else's proverbial mouth. Instead, once everyone has done what they can (even if some may be slothful), there is something that separates the bright and the dark. Not quite Fate, not quite Chance, its pips show themselves in even the smallest of ways, like this.

Even if you have no idea what may happen tomorrow, you won't decry the pips, which have come out well today.

With that, you stand up. You speak to your companions sleeping nearby on their own mounds, tell them it's morning.

"Aw, heck... Morning already?"

"You get some sleep?"

They heave themselves into consciousness, but it sounds like they didn't sleep very well. Maybe it was the battle in the dungeon, or maybe the state of the fortress city. Whichever, they seem surprised to see you looking just like normal.

You pointedly straighten your outfit, then urge the two of them to hurry up. You don't have high hopes of getting a decent meal at the tavern with the town the way it is—and there's something else you want to ask about. You want to meet with the entire party before the girls go out.

You look up, as you always do, toward the window of the economy room on the upper floor of the inn. Normally, each evening, there's a young woman who looks down at you from that window and smiles—but at this moment, there's no sign of her.

Instead, you see a slim face framed by golden hair, a different young woman looking distinctly upset as she gazes out. You try gesturing, then you try waving, and finally you call out to the girl overhead.

In a tizzy, Female Bishop opens the window and leans out dangerously far. "Y-yes? What's the matter...?!"

First, you want to meet at the door of the inn and talk about where to go from there. You outline this simple request, adding that you'd like everyone to bring their stuff with them.

"All right!" Female Bishop replies, and then she disappears back inside.

Good. You're concerned about Female Warrior, but you feel safe leaving her in the hands of Female Bishop and your cousin.

"So a group huddle, huh…?" Half-Elf Scout says when you conclude your conversation. He still looks sleepy. Then again, maybe he's just pretending. Thanks to your long acquaintance with him, you know he can be that way. Yes—it has been a long acquaintance. Not in terms of time, but long just the same.

Not just with him but with Myrmidon Monk (who's picking straw off his robes), Female Bishop, and Female Warrior, too. And your cousin, needless to say.

"…You got a plan, Captain?"

Thus when Half-Elf Scout asks this, you laugh out loud. This is no time for silly questions.

*No plan at all—hence the group huddle!*

§

You all meet in the corner of the lobby of the inn and eat the meal you got from the tavern last night. The tumult engulfing the town hasn't spared the inn; there's a crackling tension in the air. The shouts of refugees who have pushed their way inside, met by the equally vocal staff trying to keep them out, are all too easy to hear.

"What the hell do you mean, we can't stay here?! There's nowhere else *to* stay!"

"I'm very sorry, but the cots that had opened up are already taken…"

"Then put us in some other room! I know you've got plenty of 'em!"

"I'm very sorry, but we can only make the economy rooms available. If you'd like to stay in the stables—"

"You're just gonna abandon us?! Tell us to sleep with the animals?! That's bullshit!"

The inn staff had made a number of rooms available as a show of goodwill, but there were only so many people they could accommodate. Despite the burgeoning crisis, they can't just let the refugees into the fanciest suites. Even compassion doesn't mean throwing everything away for no reward. At that moment, the teachings of the temple of the Trade God were the shield that protected Order at the inn.

"...Shouldn't be surprised," Myrmidon Monk says, nodding gratefully and munching on some fruit with his mandibles. "If they threw open the doors and made the whole place available, they wouldn't have a way to *show* compassion anymore."

Money was like the roaming wind. If you stopped up the place it came from, the air would grow stagnant and foul.

You mumble your acknowledgment as you bite into a concoction of dried meat clasped between two pieces of bread, then you look around at the others. There isn't, in fact, much conversation to speak of. Your cousin is flipping through a spell book she acquired somewhere along the line, so absorbed that she almost forgets to eat. Female Warrior looks down, barely managing to get the food to her mouth, while Female Bishop watches her with concern.

Normally, Half-Elf Scout might intervene, but he seems to feel he can't act at the moment. You mutter to yourself and take a sip of the well water the staff have kindly fetched you. Even at a moment like this, cold water is delicious, and when your stomach is satisfied your nerves may feel less frayed.

*In the meantime…*

The moment you speak those words, everyone's gazes fix on you. Even Female Warrior looks at you, vacant but beseeching.

You weren't intending to say anything all that important. You give a wry smile and continue to expound. For now, the most important duty is to secure the inn.

"True enough," Half-Elf Scout says, jumping on your suggestion like it's a lifeline. He picks up the thread and runs with it, as if the conversation must not be allowed to slow. "Whatever else we're gonna do, we need somewhere we can get a decent rest."

Indeed, if you lose this base of operations, there's no telling what will become of you.

"A place to sleep, a place to rest," Female Bishop adds, nodding at the thought. "And some equipment too, right?"

"We can try to stay in an economy room, but you see this mess. Feels like someone might walk away with the cot out from under you." Half-Elf Scout glances at the people still arguing and pressing in at the entrance. You only have to think of the newbie hunters on the second floor of the dungeon to know what starving people might resort to.

Female Bishop looks disturbed, but she doesn't object. Instead, she nods. She is not some ignorant girl.

Having established that you need a base of operations, you next suggest that this is the moment to use your financial resources. That would make this an accounting issue, but your cousin, the keeper of the party's books, currently has her face buried *in* a book.

You give a little shout for your *second* cousin and her head pops up. "Huh?" she says.

Real nice. This is a matter of the party's assets, you inform her—of cash on hand. You need to know how much the group has left.

"Oh, sure… We've been careful to save up, so we've got some wiggle room." She proceeds to give you the details of the party's ledger from memory.

That settles it, then.

*'Let's rent the Royal Suite.'*

"Let's *what*?!" your cousin exclaims, at once shocked and dismayed. "You realize that'll be expensive, right? We won't be able to stay there for very long…"

Yes, but so what? There may not be very long to stay.

*How about it?* You turn toward Myrmidon Monk, who's been sitting silently with his arms folded.

"…I don't care much either way," he says gravely, then clacks his mandibles as if to indicate that's the full extent of his contribution. "If that's what you think we should do, let's do it."

"I-I'm with you…!" Female Bishop adds.

Your scout chuckles. "Beds up there are so soft, we might get older just sleepin' in 'em!"

The whole party knows the situation. The rooms on the top level will be worth the money in exchange for the safety and peace of mind they afford. Anyway, everything takes money. It will support the inn as well.

*All right.* You tell your cousin to take care of the administrative details, then start giving instructions to the rest of the party.

Although, for the most part, those instructions consist only of waiting at the inn. Losing your base would be a major blow. You'll entrust everyone else with securing that base while you go out. That, you think, will be best.

"Wha…?" Female Warrior looks at you vacantly, her eyes not quite focusing.

*You're going?* her gaze asks, and you nod. You need to get a sense of the situation in town—and whatever you do next, you need to get your equipment fixed up.

"Oh…" Female Warrior looks at the ground again. Neither of you say it, but both of you are thinking of her spear.

Half-Elf Scout takes a sidelong glance at her and says casually, "Y'know, maybe I oughtta go instead."

You shake your head no. You need someone who can let you know if anything happens at the inn. You need him to do that for you, you say.

"Well, you heard the man," replies Half-Elf Scout. "Don't do anything I wouldn't do, Cap."

*Mm.* You nod, then hand off your belongings to the others, taking only your katana as you rise to your feet. Normally, you'd rather go out in full armor, but you don't want to antagonize the refugees; it might be dangerous.

*So…*

The fortress city, it seems, is hardly different from the dungeon.

With that thought in your mind, you depart the inn.

Leaving the inn has almost always meant you're on your way to face some dangerous challenge, so your mindset is much the same as usual.

The only thing different is that you can feel Female Warrior watching you as you go, and it's distinctly uncomfortable.

§

"The hell d'you think you're doin', huh?!"

"I'm sorry! I'm sorry! I've had nothing to eat since yesterday!"

"So you thought you'd just take someone *else's* food, did you?!"

"Forgive me! I have a child to feed…!"

"And I've got *me* to feed! I risked my life for this stuff, you son of a bitch!"

The adventurer gives the weeping refugee a brutal kick, sending him sprawling across the ground. The man's child starts crying, but those around only jeer.

Everywhere you go in the fortress city there are scenes like this. Which of them is at fault? The scales of Order would probably incline toward the crime of the refugee. Dire straits cannot excuse stealing from others. Not everyone could be the priest giving a candle to the escaped prisoner, nor would it be possible to order them to do so.

The prison guard who went after the escaped convict—he was not right, but neither was he wrong. Law and Order are people's rights given to people, and as such they are imperfect, ambiguous, and expansive, and the gods see that it is good. That they are imperfect by no means implies disorder.

What is assailing the fortress city at this moment is a storm of Chaos, the panic of those people who live in terror of the shadow of death.

Making sure you can draw your katana at any time, you step into the crossroads, into the maelstrom. You wouldn't take the risk at this moment, except that that you can feel blood in the air.

"You sonuva—! Stop already!"

"Yeah, that's enough!"

After all, if you reach for the thing at your hip, or if you were to wave a magic staff around, the town guards would intervene. Or maybe they're not guards—maybe they're volunteer adventurers. Regardless, this is no time for unrestrained violence.

The new arrivals, men and women alike, fan out across the area. They aren't here to protect the townspeople from the refugees; they're here to protect everyone from the adventurers.

No matter… It won't last long.

That thought is barely through your mind as you arrive at the Golden Knight. You can already see who you're looking for inside.

"Hrm."

"H'lo."

Beside the knight in his shimmering diamond armor, a young woman with silver hair raises one hand, expressionless. Things are a little quieter here than they were the night before—maybe that's the way to describe it—no doubt because not only is the Knight of Diamonds here, but a number of dungeon-delving parties are packing the tables. The waitresses are sweeping up sawdust that was put down to soak up blood.

*Looks like those refugees learned a very hard lesson.*

That's not the only reason the tavern seems so on edge despite the midday hour, though. The knight's party carries armfuls of baggage and exudes menace.

*'Planning to flee the city?'*

The Knight of Diamonds responds to your jocular greeting with "Something like that," flashing a pained smile. He gives his party some instructions with a lordly air, then beckons to you and leaves the table. Only the silver-haired scout follows him, falling into line behind you.

You're grateful for this, it must be said. This is not something you wish just anyone to overhear.

"So… I take it from your look that something happened to you. Care to fill me in?"

*Mm.* You nod.

The worst possible outcome would be if, on top of everything else, you and your party were to disappear down in the darkness and take everything you know with you to your graves. You know you must tell someone what you've learned, immediately; ideally, the other party you trust the most. There is no point in telling some half-baked crew of adventurers; it has to be someone of proven mettle, someone you have faith in.

Here in the fortress city, where ranks and tags have no meaning, the only basis for such faith is how many floors a group has descended.

In other words, the Knight of Diamonds and his people are the only ones.

The man who waits in the innermost chamber of the Death, red blade in hand. The source of all this evil; the Dungeon Master.

The route to the fifth floor, the elevator to the abyss. The path you've found, be it by Fate or Chance.

All of this you tell the Knight of Diamonds, calmly, sticking to only what he needs to know. The young woman's eyes widen—in surprise or horror, you're not sure—but the diamond knight seems impressed. He listens to you in silence, then there's a beat, and after a moment he says, "I see." He pauses again, then adds, "If that's the case, then we should go down and behead that bastard straightaway. But…"

*But we can't do that?*

"…sadly, we can't." The Knight of Diamonds sighs. "If the leaders of our nation don't do something about this, no one will. I don't know whether it's the end of the world, but it's certainly the end of our land."

He's exactly right about that. You are no merchant. You can't even keep track of your party's finances. But as its leader, you've handled a fair amount of cash. The fortress city is overflowing with loot. Treasure wells up endlessly from the dungeon.

But that's all it does.

The money swells up like a bubble, and the price of everything goes up. There is no ceiling. Eventually, no matter how many riches you have, there will be nothing left to buy. Food, clothing, will all disappear until there's only money, adventurers, and the Death.

It seems like a situation in which the king should act. But judging from the state of the city…

"He's only interested in saving his own skin at this point," the Knight of Diamonds spits. "As long as his lavish palace is in one piece, he doesn't care. It's foolishness."

The silver-haired girl goggles at him—but you agree. The only thing supporting Order in the fortress city at this moment is the wind the Trade God's temple blows through the area. There can be no free acts of goodwill—or if there are, it would be wrong to force them. Without that teaching saturating the city, the refugees would be allowed to eat everyone out of house and home in the name of compassion.

It's the merchants attempting to uphold that Order—the merchants, and the guards, as well as the adventurers. They have gathered in this city, survived the dungeon; they are given nothing from outside. From outside come only people with starvation and thirst and nothing else to their names. People who take their circumstances as an excuse to steal from others, or people who lurk down in the dungeon; they are both the same.

In the end, there's only one way to survive in the fortress city: hack and slash.

All will sink ultimately into Chaos. Even if someone did slay the Dungeon Master, it would mean nothing.

All that there is, is the Death.

"I'm going to kill him," the Knight of Diamonds says. You look at him. There is no laughter in his eyes; this is no joke. He is absolutely serious. "He's a Vampire Lord already, entranced by the Death."

Who is "he"? Even you can tell.

Nearby, the silver-haired girl looks from you to the knight and back, ill at ease.

"I'm going to chop off his head, I'm going to take command of this country, and then I'm going to push back against the Army of Darkness. However…"

*Victory would be meaningless if the world is still suffused with the Death.*

"What I'm saying is you and I share the same interests here. What do you think?"

There is one hope: to cut this evil off at the root.

The knight smiles at you, the smile of a mischievous child, and your own expression is much the same. You nod. No hesitation. That is, after all, why you came to this place, even back in the beginning.

"I'm not about to let some No-Life King have his way in the capital. I'm going into that evil grotto."

*And when the Dungeon Master's head goes flying, everything will be over.*

You share another nod. It's all you need.

You were truly fortunate to make this man's acquaintance.

"With that settled, I do have one favor to ask you."

*By all means.*

"It's this young lady." He places a hand on the silver-haired girl's shoulder, but at first, you're not sure of his intentions. She looks at her leader, as confused as you are, but then he continues. "The rest of us, we were like this from the start. But the girl came later. She was caught up in things, you might say."

He's probably about to ask you to take her on as part of your party, or so you suspect. But she's faster than he is.

"…I'm going with you," she says. She speaks softly, and yet you feel as if she shouted. She brushes away the diamond knight's gauntlet with a slim hand, then looks him right in the eye and insists, "I absolutely will not be left behind…!"

You and this girl don't know each other all that well. You have no idea what road she and the Knight of Diamonds have walked together, what adventures they've been on. Just as he and she don't know about you and your party's adventures.

You can see, however, the tears in the girl's eyes, the way she grits her teeth, the force of will that causes her to insist on accompanying him. How could you miss them?

"I'm your scout. No one else's. That was my choice that I made by myself. *For* myself."

*Doesn't look like you can shake this one.*

You don't have to say it—the Knight of Diamonds gives an awkward scratch of his cheek, then sighs, the gesture and the sound more eloquent than any other answer he could give.

You grin in spite of yourself, and that's when the silver-haired girl turns to you. This time she says, "There *is* someone I want you to take care of. The girl."

You nod, accepting her request.

You had always intended to do everything you could.

The silver-haired girl's cheeks soften at your answer, then she gives you a sort of exasperated smile and says, "I knew it would be something like that."

§

"Spear, huh? That's a tough one."

Down in the grimy hole that is the weapon shop is an old man so small, so curled into himself, that you could mistake him for a dwarf. He strokes his chin and shoots you an unenthused look. You were asking him about Female Warrior's broken spear, but his answer doesn't sound promising.

"Most people who go down in the dungeon, they want a sword at their side, or a mace—or a staff." He casts a glance around the shop; you follow suit and see that most of the merchandise is of those varieties. Broadswords, pulverizing hammers, padfoot killers, and mage slayers. Not much resembling a spear. When you do spot the rare polearm, it inspires a look on your face not much more pleased than that on the owner's.

"Mass-produced trinkets, all of 'em. Break after a few good hits. Not terrible products, but not what you'd call superior weaponry."

You cross your arms and mumble that you were afraid of this.

They say an accomplished warrior can fight with any weapon, but that doesn't mean they *should*. It doesn't help that you're not shopping for yourself, but for your comrade. You want something suited to her expertise, if you can find it. The man in black broke her last spear—so at the very least, she needs something stronger than that, or there may be no point at all. In which case, she will have to either acquire a new weapon outside the fortress city or get one smithed up here.

"With things the way they are...," the owner says, "it's not impossible." But it's obvious that the chances of a successful roll are agonizingly small.

There are times when it's acceptable, even necessary, to stake your life on a roll of the dice—but now is not that time.

*So it's difficult to find a superior spear in the fortress city at this moment?*

"I can try to look, and I will, but it won't come cheap."

You would be grateful, even for that. If anything, you'd worry if it didn't cost much.

There's one other thing...

"That sword of yours?"

*Mm.* You nod, taking your weapon, scabbard and all, from your hip. It's nameless but sharp. Trustworthy. Though whether it can stand you in good stead against that red blade and the man in black who wields it, you don't know.

It's gotten you this far, you suppose.

When that red blade was in the hand of the young magic warrior, this sword was indeed a match for it. Perhaps, then, it can be counted upon in the next battle as well.

"All right, I'll take care of it," the owner says. You pluck a gold coin from your purse, purchase a medley of consumables, and then squeeze your way out of the cramped den.

The suffocating claustrophobia, however, doesn't go away when you reach street level. The sensation, the feeling of the wind that blows through the crossroads among the close-packed stone buildings is different somehow. The square of sky overhead seems farther away than it did before, and the townspeople's voices don't reach your ears.

Instead, all you can hear is the arguing of the adventurers and the refugees; all you can feel is the tension; all you can smell is the ever-present Death.

For just a second, you even fancy that you're down in the depths, exploring the dungeon. Will there come a day when the buildings of the four corners look like nothing more than wire frame to you?

That will be the day you're no different from those bushwhackers.

With a faint chuckle, you are about to set off with your purchases when:

"…It's not easy being you, eh?"

A familiar voice blows to you on the pleasant wind, and you stop.

*It's her.*

A small woman crouches, smiling like a cat in the shadows of the buildings just at the edge of the street. Grinning from under her cloak, the informant trots toward you.

Well, she's right—times are tough. Whether they're much tougher than usual, you're not sure about.

"Hmm?"

For what you must do hasn't changed, not one bit.

When you tell her so, the informant goes quiet with an expression difficult to describe. She stares at you, her lips a single, taut line. You fold your arms and wait for a response.

Each time she appears, it's because she has something she wants to tell you. And what she tells you has always come in useful. She seems to change the very situation around you, as if sending up a signal flag.

So today, you resolve to hear what she has to say.

"…I don't think things are going to just conveniently go your way," she murmurs after a moment, sounding somehow tired. "People aren't that smart, and the ones who think they're smart just waste their time yammering. There might not even be any help, eh?"

Yes, well, that's about the long and short of it. You meet her probing gaze with unhesitating agreement.

That's the way people are. No big deal. But it's not worthless, either. It just is what it is. One doesn't blot out the other—much as many people are prone to flit between different extremes.

Therefore, you tell her, you intend to do exactly what you can. If it proves futile, so it goes. You have no interest in placing blame on others, yet neither will it be your fault if the world is destroyed.

Adventurers commuting between the first chamber and the surface like ash that comes from no fire; you yourself, bulling ahead, chasing a Death that might not even be there.

There's no big difference between the two. Perhaps only the sense of self-satisfaction in your respective hearts.

You repeat with a shrug that this is the way things are—that's enough.

"_____"

For a moment the informant stares at you, wide-eyed and seemingly speechless. She looks almost as awed as she does exasperated. Beneath the hood of her cloak, her lips curl into a smile like the bud of a flower, and she lets out a breath. "Well. Looks like there's no stopping you."

*So it seems.*

You agree easily, not thinking much of it.

"In that case, take my advice and drop by the temple of the Trade God."

You echo: *'The temple?'*

"That's right. The temple," she replies. "I find that at moments like this, it never hurts to ask the gods for a friendly boost. You can never have too much help."

You realize you agree with her. Besides, you think maybe you should see that nun one more time. This might be the last.

"...Yeah, maybe," the informant says after a moment of silence. "Might be a good idea." With that, she slips past you and starts off down the street. Two steps, three, almost as if she's dancing; next, she turns back toward you with a swirl of her cloak. "The Trade God is the patron of meetings and travel! Take your time getting there!"

Then she's gone with the wind, leaving behind only a faint aroma.

You look vacantly up at the sky over the fortress city. That cutout piece of air still looks far away—but a little closer than before. Has the sky come down a little closer to you, or have you climbed up toward it? Who can say?

You entertain these silly thoughts as you amble in the direction of the temple. You don't have much time, but then, you never do. It's precisely at moments like this that you need to slow down and enjoy the walk. Nothing wrong with that.

To live is freedom. You can do as you like until the moment you encounter the Death.

§

The temple of the Trade God is the last bastion of justice in the fortress city.

Refugees press in, as do those who have been robbed by refugees.

The temple takes in all but spits back out those who, in the name of goodwill, seek protection and compassion at no price.

Of course, compensation is sought from those who are accepted within the temple grounds: save others, as you have been saved. Do a bit of cleaning or cooking, be it ever so humble, and if you cannot do those things, do what you can. Like money, goodwill flows among people: a pleasant breeze.

*But even so, there are limits.*

Goodwill does not come from nothing. It is born of the heart. Something is always needed to fill the heart—and that thing is nearly gone now.

Soon all will be in tatters.

The clerics of the Trade God, however, bustle back and forth in a way that betrays none of this. They look like people at prayer, and they minister to believers.

You take all this in as you climb the long staircase to the temple.

Everything seems poised precariously, one step from the edge of a cliff. One large step, though the precipice looms.

Only the relentless effort of those who have dug in their heels is maintaining Order at this moment.

You climb silently past the line of supplicating refugees. When you look up, you see puffing smoke, although this is not some dragon's mountain home.

The molten earth under that mountain isn't inexhaustible. One day, the cauldron will still, and the smoke will cease.

At this moment, however, that's your guidepost, and you expect it to be for some time.

You climb the stairs. With each step you take, you hear the metallic *click* of sabbatons behind you.

You continue forward. The sound comes again. You jump a stair. So does the sound. You stop, and the sound stops, too.

*Well.*

That certainly does make the sound seem very deliberate. Intentional.

You think for a moment, and then ultimately without really thinking at all you offer: *'Want to climb to the temple together?'*

The *click* comes again, louder than before. You stop and wait.

"......"

In lieu of an answer, footsteps walk up beside you. You glance to the side and find hair as dark as a damp crow bobbing by your shoulder.

*'Weren't you looking after the inn?'*

You try your best not to make it sound like a rebuke, but she still flinches. You scratch your chin, wondering if you've made a mistake. As gently as possible, you ask if she told the others she was coming.

"...Mm," she responds with a bob of her head. You're sure it was a nod, albeit a subtle one.

She's clutching the broken haft of her spear to her ample chest. To the uninformed observer, it might look like nothing more than a ruined weapon, but you, you understand what it means.

With a word of encouragement, you start up the steps. Hesitantly, the sabbatons click out beside you.

A couple instances, you pass adventurers coming down the stairs with vacant expressions. A couple more, adventurers rush up the stairs past you, a party member cradled in their arms. Some of the refugees waiting for food open their mouths to complain, then shut them again at the air of urgency.

Adventurers who walk side by side with the Death are going to the temple. No one would dare get in their way. Whatever may be happening beyond the city walls, what goes on in the dungeon hasn't changed. Not a bit.

*That includes us.*

"…?"

The thought brings a smile to your face for some reason, and it's only then that you notice Female Warrior watching you with a questioning look.

You shake your head and tell her it's nothing. You exhale.

"…I thought so," Female Warrior murmurs at that moment. "We're going, aren't we?"

She doesn't say where. She doesn't need to: You're both adventurers.

Before you can answer, she comes to a halt and grabs your sleeve, tugging hard.

The violet eyes you see just a step below you are damp, wavering; they look ready to overflow at any moment.

"You know…we might…die down there."

You respond without hesitation that yes, you might. In fact, there seems a very good chance.

"Then why—?!"

People die. It is what they do.

Every person, of every kind. You yourself. Those people over there.

In this, you are all the same.

A smart person would probably be able to come up with a host of reasons to avoid this fight. Then they would mock you, eager to show how much more intelligent they are than you.

Just as you used to, when you looked with contempt at the adventurers who stayed on the first floor of the dungeon.

That contempt, however, is now gone from your heart.

Is it because every day, morning and evening, you have hardened yourself against the prospect of death, the knowledge that you might die today or tomorrow?

It's funny—it's only now, when things have turned so serious, that your heart is calm, like a still lake.

There's no difference between those who wander the first level of the dungeon and those who seek to delve its darkest depths.

You will challenge the Death. In that, there is no change at all.

You fight, you kill, you win, you survive, you go on to the next thing. Or you "go to 14," and end up dead as a coffin nail.

That's all there is.

You are an unclouded blade.

A keen weapon pointed at the enemy.

You are a spark, burning brightly.

Therefore, you tell her, you *want* her to come with you, but you will not—cannot—order her to do so.

"…!"

Female Warrior bites her lip. Her bleary eyes narrow in a glare.

If you indeed ordered her to accompany you, she would probably offer a smart remark, but she would come. That was what she was hoping for, and you know that. You understand.

But that isn't right. Your reason comes from within yourself, not from within her.

She was robbed of her name at birth, forced to adventure against her will.

Her family and friends went into the dungeon, and so she went with them.

To save her lost sisters, she sought out the Death.

All that is meaningless now. She doesn't have one single reason to risk her life adventuring.

With the money she's made to this point, it would be easy to buy her freedom.

It's impossible to resurrect her sisters. And in the deep depths of the dungeon, all that waits is the reeking Death.

She has no reason to try herself against the dungeon.

"E-everyone else…"

They're all going. Well, most likely—you laugh.

You're sure that Female Bishop, like you, will clutch her sword and scales and get to her feet. This has been her lifelong duty. She knows already why she lives and why she may die. She won't abandon the fight against the Death, you suspect, if only to make sure her friends can rest in peace.

She's no different at all from when she was an identifier.

Your cousin is the same. She might get on your nerves, the way she treats you like a little brother, but you know she's coming from a good place. Now that you know the man in black is using magic for evil ends to spread the Death, that he used the source of the evil that afflicts this world—you now know you are the ones who can do something about it, who must do something about it. Or anyway, so you figure your cousin thinks.

As for Half-Elf Scout: He's lighthearted, cowardly, and facetious. But you also recognize that he's always the one who risks himself against the treasure chests; that he fights a lonely fight for the party's fate. He can rely on no one else to fight it, yet he keeps winning. He is a brave, strong adventurer. You're sure he's as good as his word: He's in this dungeon to lop off the head of the Dungeon Master. Whether he wants fame, fortune, or whatever else from it, he risks his own life, and that makes him an adventurer.

Then there's Myrmidon Monk. What about him? He's the most mysterious member of your party—or at least, you never quite seem to know what he's thinking. But there's also no doubt in your mind that he is a man to be relied upon. He may say he doesn't care either way, but whenever there's dangerous exploring to be done, he's with you. You suspect he will be again. "I really don't care either way," he'll clack, and then down he'll go into the depths of the dungeon. You don't know if it's faith or some unique way of thinking that the myrmidons possess, but for you, *that's* something that doesn't matter either way. His resolution is always clear and firm.

With all that in mind…

'What will you do?'

"M-me…?" Female Warrior is unable to answer. She looks up at you, still clutching her spear, then drops her gaze to her feet.

She's a child about to be stranded on her own, told that if she doesn't hurry up, she'll be left behind. Just a little girl.

True, she may very well decide to go down into the dungeon purely because everyone else is going, too. She'll fight the monsters. Even gripped by the fear of slimes—no, gripped by the fear of the Death, she'll fight.

But that wouldn't be right. It can't be. When she finally died, if it happened like that, no one would be happy. Not her—and not you.

"Not...you?" she asks.

That's right.

You, as party leader, are entrusted with the lives of all your party's members. You feel a responsibility if someone dies. It's not something you can shrug off by saying *These things happen.* It doesn't matter if it was just a bad roll on the dice of Fate and Chance; it will feel like your fault.

And yet, despite that, death is the outcome.

Your companions chose their own adventure, and this was the result.

If you feel responsibility for that, that's your problem. You have your own adventure.

It doesn't change the fact that your party member died at the end of theirs.

Whatever the outcome of that adventure, all you can do is accept it. No one can fight it.

But what if, instead... What if it wasn't an adventure?

What if it was someone who simply tagged along with you, who wouldn't have died if you had only told her to stay home?

That would not, in the end, be something you could accept.

And so you say to her that if she is to journey into the dungeon, if she is to challenge the Death that lies in the deepest depths known to this world, then you want her to do it for her own sake, by her own volition, for the adventure.

"M-me...?" Her shoulders are shaking. Her slim, elegant shoulders; the shoulders of a young woman. "What I want..." The violet eyes waver, droplets falling from them, running down her cheeks.

The sabbatons step forward, hesitantly but at the same time full of volition.

"I want…I want to be…with you!"

With her next step, she veritably flings herself at you, collapsing into your chest, clasping you, pitching forward—it is the greatest step she can take.

She weeps as if she has no other way to communicate that she doesn't want you to die.

"Is that…is that not enough?!"

Some passersby stop and look on with interest, but you couldn't care less. It's all you can do to place a hand on the shoulder of the woman crying into your chest, to brush her hair.

*Never intended…*

To make her say anything like that.

Lost between yes and no—but let us be clear, not frustrated by this—you gaze up at the sky. It looks strange—or, perhaps, ordinary. Blue and clear as far as the eye can see.

Whatever may happen on the board, the blue of the sky never changes; the sun and the twin moons and the stars will continue in their rounds.

No, no—even to say the sky is blue shows how narrow your vision is. The sky isn't *just* blue. It turns red sometimes, or purple. And sometimes it's dim. Black. A rich, velvety darkness.

All those times when she visited you, when you chatted together—those times, the sky was ensconced in the curtain of night. It's strange, to realize that the night sky seems a deep violet to you. Maybe it's the lights of the town. It's the color of her hair.

You let out a breath. You can feel the small tremors of her body through your palms.

Yes, the sky you look up at right now is blue, somehow congratulatory. The wind blows, making the windmill creak. You say:

'*How could it not be enough?*'

How could anything not be enough?

If that's what she wishes, if that's what she's decided, then that is her adventure. You cannot, and would not, speak against it.

At that, she continues to stare at the ground for a moment, then rubs her eyelids and looks up at you.

"…Hmph. You!" she says softly. She manages to work a small smile onto her face. The violet eyes gaze at you. "Making a girl embarrass herself like that... You're going to make it up to me, you hear?"

There's no more intimidating place to make a commitment like that than before the temple of the Trade God, patron of merchantry and promises.

Your response evokes a whisper of "Dummy," and a jab in your side. Then she takes your hand.

She's already looking pointedly away as her fingers intertwine with yours.

You laugh out loud. You laugh, and then you start climbing the stairs. Slowly, surely, one step at a time.

As you crest the top of the stairs, the long climb finally over, a shadow falls on you.

"...And what exactly do you think you're doing in front of my temple? Unbelievable."

It's a devout believer running her hand through her hair—which is a mess, as if she ran to get here.

§

"I've got a general idea of what's going on, but insofar as I really had to rush, I hope you'll remember to be grateful." The nun who ushered you into the worship hall has stern words as she leads you to the altar. Perhaps this is her way of saying she shouldn't have wasted her energy worrying about you. You decide not to ask.

Even the temple of the Trade God can't entirely escape the repercussions of the Chaos that presses in on the town. People are crouched here and there in the stone building, groaning from their wounds, crying from their hunger, or howling with lament for lost loved ones.

A significant number of them have no doubt come here knowing that it is their last lifeline. Even adventurers fresh from the dungeon know better than to fight with the refugees here.

*No... Perhaps it's more than that.*

Perhaps it's that all those who give alms and seek salvation are equal before the Trade God. It is a tremendous thing, you think, and fearsome.

How many times has your own heart wavered during your adventures exploring the dungeon? The nun puffs out her well-formed chest proudly, as if to say her own heart of faith has never been shaken. "So. What brings you here today?" she asks.

"The...the girls. My sisters." You leave it to Female Warrior, beside you, to stumblingly form the words. These words are not for you to speak. Instead, you accept her squeeze of your hand, so hard it hurts. "I want you to...bury them."

"..." The nun blinks several times. "You're quite sure?"

"N-no, but...yes." Female Warrior's expression is unreadable; with her free hand—the one that isn't holding yours—she brushes the haft of her spear.

You find yourself remembering a haggard woman lying in a hut. She looks exactly as she always has, like she might get up and move at any moment, but there is no life in her. That makes her no different from any other object, and yet you're sad to lose her from the world. It's hard for you to admit that her loss will change not one single thing about the way the world works. In a few years, no trace of her worth speaking of will be left. Those are the facts.

You don't know whether it was right of you to bury your master. Was it the right choice to bury her, request services from the local temple, and then set out on your journey?

Sometimes you wonder. As you wonder at this moment.

"I'm not sure, but...I need...I need to say good-bye."

As for Female Warrior, perhaps she will regret this choice later, but for now, she has given her answer. She will part ways with her sisters, her former party members; she will stop looking back at the Death and the Life, and move forward.

The nun accepts her gaze: weak, broken, but still facing forward. "...I see," she says, her response mercilessly brief. She speaks in a tone of voice that could be taken in almost any way, but there's a hint of warmth there, in her near-absolute-zero look...

"You have a donation ready, yes? Then come this way, please," she says.

*All right. Just imagining it, maybe.*

"...Yeah," Female Warrior whispers, and then, not without regret, she lets go of your hand.

The nun leads her deeper into the temple, and you watch her go. If she had held on to your hand, you would probably be going with her. But she didn't.

Instead, you mingle with the other adventurers in the worship hall and wait for her.

There are times when you want someone to understand you, times when you want support—and there are times when you need to deal with something alone. At this moment, she has entrusted you with waiting for her, and it is not your place to reject her.

You look up at the symbol of the Trade God raised high above the worship hall. Despite the considerable confusion within the hall, it somehow feels severe and silent.

That makes you think: Until now, you've never spent much time here in the middle of the day. The longest stretch you've spent at this temple was the night when you yourself wandered on the border between life and death.

You brush the scar on your neck unconsciously, your eyes fixed on the symbol of the Trade God, shaped like a windmill.

Prayer is not a thing that you know. You think it's very impure to pray in the hopes that your wish will come true. Yet you also think that if one were to pray, *knowing* such a prayer is impure, might the gods not acknowledge such a prayer as pure?

If the gods could not heed such a prayer, they would be derided as useless, as evil, as villains.

How small a thing you are! How selfish and prideful!

Hence, you decide not to pray.

Instead, you resolve to describe and report roughly where you have been and where you are going. Not forgetting to add that, if the gods are not too busy, perhaps they might lend you a hand. If you're going to ask for help, why hide it? Why not just ask?

To ask of the gods, to request of the deities—there can't be any harm in doing it, just in case. You need all the help you can get.

You close your eyes and think of all of it. Communicate all of it. Give it over to them. Then, slowly, you open your eyes.

You find yourself still looking at the windmill symbol of the Trade God.

Well, naturally enough.

How many adventurers do you think there are in the Four-Cornered World praying to the Trade God, asking for help? You can hardly expect the god to focus on you alone. The best you can hope for is that perhaps, when you really need it, you might get some modicum of assistance of some kind you hadn't imagined.

You don't forget to grab some coins from your wallet and offer them on the altar. This town has taught you well: No request is answered for free.

"Well, aren't you devout?"

"..."

It seems more time has passed than you realized. The nun has reappeared behind you and fixed you with her cold gaze. Female Warrior stands beside her, sniffling. She's no longer holding her spear.

*'All good?'*

"No, but...yes," she whispers, much as she did before, and shakes her head. It sends a gentle ripple through her dark hair. She smiles and says, "I'm going to make something good of it."

*Ah* is all you say. However, things are not entirely problem free.

"Wha...?" Female Warrior's eyes widen with unease, and you point out in utter seriousness that she has no weapon. "Oh... Y-yeah. *That.* Sheesh." She pouts a little—but this is a grave matter.

She needs a weapon, one suited to her skills and fit for delving the dungeon's deepest depths. You asked the guy at the weapon shop for one, but you doubt he'll procure it in time. If push comes to shove, maybe you can have some old sword converted into a long-handled blade or what have you.

"Tell me something," the nun says with a discreet cough. She gives you a look of curiosity, as if this is no more than intriguing gossip to her. "May I take this to mean you're going back down into the dungeon?"

You speak the word *yes* as if nothing could be simpler.

Now that you think about it, nothing could. Long ago, very long ago, you resolved to face the depths of the dungeon. It seems so obvious in this moment.

When and why did you decide? Maybe you already knew from the day you came to the fortress city, or maybe your feelings have simply been numbed as you work your way through the dungeon. In any case, it's not as if something has abruptly changed between yesterday and today—it just is what it is. Simple fact.

There is a place unknown, a threat unknown, monsters unknown—and beyond them, the Dungeon Master.

What you must do hasn't changed.

The nun listens to your answer, then closes her eyes and is silent for a moment. At length, she says, "So—you too, Miss?"

"…Yes," Female Warrior says, quiet but firm.

The nun sighs defeatedly. "Then I think you should take this." She offers something to Female Warrior: a long object wrapped in purple felt.

Female Warrior reaches out, hesitant, and takes it. It appears light in her hands. "May I look at it…?" she asks.

"Well, yes. I wouldn't have given it to you otherwise."

Female Warrior pulls away the cloth, revealing…

"A wooden…spear…?"

That's right: a spear. Polished and carved from tip to hilt, a wooden weapon that could almost be mistaken for the real thing. Yet it's such a superlative weapon that Female Warrior unconsciously sighs to see it.

"It's a hardwood spear," the nun informs her. "Made of oak and blessed."

"Is this the holy…?"

"It's modeled after the holy spear, the one the blind sage gave to the warrior who would harrow the dark fortress."

That makes sense. From that perspective, it certainly is appropriate for your party's warrior. Knowing how faithful your bishop is, it wouldn't surprise you if one day she's hailed as a holy woman.

"To be clear, this isn't the real holy spear," the nun says, looking at you. "But it was blessed by the hand of a sage just the same. I think it can help you."

*'A sage?'*

"That would be me. What of it?"

You can't help but smile at her laconic response.

Ah, this must indeed be a wondrous and wonderworking weapon, then. Surely nothing compares.

*'How about it?'*

"Give me a second…"

There's a *thump*—Female Warrior's sabbatons striking the floor of the worship hall and launching her as they did many times before. The blade of the oak spear whistles through the air, cutting through the darkness, stabbing at empty space. It already looks comfortable in her hands; it responds to her movements like a living thing. The spear seems to leap on its own, it almost looks like it's dancing with Female Warrior.

The eyes of people in the worship hall begin to focus on Female Warrior; people who had hung their heads helplessly or had been lost in prayer. Female Warrior and the oak spear appear among them like a miracle.

There could be few weapons more valuable, even those from the hand of a storied master.

"It's wonderful. I think it's…wonderful," she says as the dance ends. She holds the spear close to her ample chest with both hands. It's just how she looked when you came to the temple, and yet different.

That is, when you came to the temple moments ago—and long ago.

You suddenly wonder when that was; you try to remember the first time you encountered her. Female Warrior's movements were so light footed back then. Looking back, you realize it was born of a desire never to go backward.

Completely different from how she moved just now.

"The dead are not beside us, nor is the Death something to be despised," the nun intones to you and to Female Warrior, who is holding the hardwood spear. Or rather, the nun is speaking to all those gathered here in the temple of the Trade God. She's dispensing divine teaching. "Thoughts, feelings, life, death—all travel, all come and go."

So too pain, fortune, joy, sorrow. So too the thoughts of the dead. So too the prayers of the living.

"Therefore the wind is by your side, and will be, so long as you journey."

©lack

"Yes…" The delicate smile is hardly on Female Warrior's face before you dip your head to the Trade God, and to the nun.

If you cannot be grateful for this, when will you ever be grateful?

*Yes… It's always worth asking.*

§

"Yo, Captain! Got a few tidbits for you!"

Upon your return, you're greeted by your scout, who's sitting cross-legged on the plush bed. You and Female Warrior, who's still hugging the oak spear, share a look when you hear the jovial note in his voice.

"Turns out, way back when, that place used to be a proving ground or a treasure store or somethin'. Went a whole ten floors down." He watches you both closely as he continues explaining. "They say—they *say*, mind you…"

What's now known as the Dungeon of the Dead was built as a proving ground, a labyrinth to help a king of old choose his soldiers by putting them through trial after trial. That room on the fourth floor was the final test; what's beyond it is unclear. A treasure hoard, maybe, or else some other important room…

"Couldn't dig up anything else, though. No idea what the dude in black's been up to down there."

Your scout doesn't claim that he doesn't know, but that he couldn't find out. Rather than relying on half-baked assumptions, it will be much safer for you to go in with the mindset that you're stepping into *terra incognita*, a place unknown.

You can agree with that—but that's not the part that surprises you. You want to know how your scout came by all this information about the dungeon without ever leaving the inn. Did he hear it from some adventurers who ducked into the establishment trying to get away from the ruckus outside—or perhaps he heard it from a royal guard who came to make sure things were staying calm around here?

Half-Elf Scout sees you looking at him and waves his hand in a gesture you know well by now. "You want to catch a wolf, ask the pack," he says. You sigh. So even the infamous Bandits Guild has set up shop in this city.

*All right. More important things.*

Does this mean he plans to go?

"Sure. If you do, Cap." He gives you a smile, seemingly unconcerned. You find yourself oddly embarrassed that he saw through you so easily, not that you were trying to hide anything. "Pretty sure the lady there feels the same way. Can't be slackin' then, can I?"

Female Warrior looks pointedly away, as if to say that this is perfectly ordinary. It seems she feels the same way. She won't quite look at you, either; instead, she strides into the room on her long legs. She's going for a corner of the luxurious chamber, toward someone sitting next to your cousin (who has her face buried in a spell book, completely absorbed). Female Bishop.

Female Bishop was playing with her blue ribbon, but when she senses Female Warrior sitting down beside her, she looks up. "Are you…okay?" she asks.

"…Yeah," Female Warrior says, giving her a small nod. "What about you?"

"Me, I…"

That's the last of their conversation you really hear; you make it your business not to catch the rest. Female Bishop isn't speaking to you, and anyway, you know she's the kind to move forward. So instead you go over to Myrmidon Monk, whose massive frame dwarfs the sumptuous chair he's sitting in.

He breaks his cross-armed silence long enough to wave his antennae and say, "I don't care either way," after which he closes his mandibles with a *clack*.

*Hoh.* Casual as anything, you sit down across from him and look into his face with its unreadable expression. You've known him for more than just a short while now. You don't have to be able to read his expression to know what he's feeling.

"I heard the rumors that the royal capital is in a bad way, too. Something about a Vampire Lord."

You nod the affirmative. After all, the Knight of Diamonds never said not to tell anyone, which implies that the quick-eared already know.

Still, there's no pleasure in talking much about that No-Life King, the literal ruler of the dead.

"The Army of Darkness. The uproar in this city. Hoarding treasure from the dungeon. Seems there's a fair few things going on," Myrmidon Monk says.

*Mm.* The world is indeed in danger. Still, there are those who continue just the same with their daily toil. Some of them might want to raise the money to use Resurrection on their comrades. Others, to support their family. Still others, to eat good food, drink good drink, play at leisure, and live a life of ease.

To those ends they go down in the depths, returning to the surface with loot and nothing more. Are their adventures less than yours? No, no they're not.

Just because an adventure is about saving the world doesn't make it worth more.

To think so would make you no different from that young magic warrior and their party, wouldn't it? No different from the man in black controlling them.

For that reason, Myrmidon Monk's words sink deep inside you.

"I'm okay either way. I don't care where we go. I'm versatile. The day I lose that versatility is the day I cease to exist."

However… When you hear him, you deliberately adopt a grim look, crossing your arms and even throwing in a groan for good measure. Sounds like you and the others will be the only ones facing the depths of the Dungeon of the Dead.

"…Fine. Twist my arm," Myrmidon Monk says, his mandibles clacking. You're almost certain it's what passes for laughter with him.

In order to maintain his versatility, he has to go. That's what he claims, at least, and you respond with a nod. Sure. No choice at all.

"I'm going!" someone chirps from the corner of the room—your cousin, who has extricated herself from her book. She doesn't actually look up; her focus simply seems to snap to the present moment, her voice easy and light. "Don't forget me. I'm going, too!"

That's the extent of what she tells you. Then her mind is right back in the sea of letters, once more seeking the words of true power.

*Didn't really have to tell me at all.*

You hardly have to think to know why she's focused so hard. So you reply, simply, that you understand. That's enough to settle the point.

"A-and me, too…!" Female Bishop says anxiously, and her words are not much more surprising than your cousin's. You hesitate to point out that it's the same face she made on coming back from the dungeon; consider it a show of faith in your cousin. The very fact that your cousin can focus on her own pursuits is proof that Female Bishop is able to stand on her own two feet and make her own choices. "I'm going… I have to."

She squeezes the blue ribbon tight, like it's the hand of a precious friend. She drops her sightless gaze to the ground for an instant, then fixes it firmly on you. "Because that's why I came to this city."

Her words are strong and clear, a declaration of her will. She will not be shaken.

What reason could you possibly have to doubt her? She's on her way to becoming a hero.

Lastly, your eyes settle on Female Warrior, who crouches beside Female Bishop. She holds the oak spear and looks up at you.

"…Yeah," she says with a nod and a little smile. "Shall we go?"

*Well then.* You tell them that settles it.

These six people are going to save the world.

§

Once adventurers make a decision, they are quick to act. It takes only a day for each of you to prepare your equipment, your consumables, your provisions, potions, and everything else you need. Meanwhile, you take the opportunity to let the man at the armor shop know what happened with the spear; you pick up your sword and leave an apology.

"Think I did good work here," the man says and offers you your weapon. You take it with a respectful word, draw it from the sheath, and have a look.

*Yes. Fine work indeed.*

The sword hasn't been reborn. It's the same faithful blade to which you've entrusted your life all this time in the dungeon, meaning you can trust it again in the next battle. Such is its edge—it's a fine blade.

"Whether you win or not, that depends on how you use it," the armorer says as you inspect the sword. Then he adds, "But you've got one thing the other guy doesn't."

Well, what might that be? You give him a curious look, and he grins.

"A decent smith and polisher! They don't have one of those in the bowels of the Dungeon of the Dead, I can promise you that!"

He's right. Yes, truer words were never spoken.

You offer your thanks amidst the armorer's laughter and then slide the sword into your belt. The familiar weight of the large and small blades is comforting—it roots you somehow. It says to you this is as things should be.

*Even though skill is not lessened by the lack of a weapon or enhanced by the possession thereof.*

A passing thought, and then you work your way along the bustling street, almost swimming through the crowd. You reach the inn—and there they are. Standing ready, or with a book open, or leaning patiently against a wall, waiting for you.

When Female Warrior spots you, she gives the butt of her oaken spear a good kick, twirling it around in her hand. "Took your sweet time, didn't you?"

"Now everything's ready!" Female Bishop clenches one hand into a fist and squeezes the sword and scales with the other.

Beside her, your cousin puffs out her chest and adds, "Ready and waiting!"

You look to Myrmidon Monk for confirmation, and he doesn't say anything; he waves his antennae in the affirmative.

In that case, best to go. You nod to him, and then you lead the party out into the fortress city.

The city is still lively, still bustling—but the atmosphere has changed. It's no longer talk of adventure that people trade as easily as the weather, but talk of the world's danger. The vivacious spirit that circulates along with the loot is gone; grim, downcast faces line the roads, refugees crouching with vacant eyes.

You hear yelling, angry voices, adventurers arguing with these people. Each time the sounds reach your ears, Female Bishop looks up. She glances back several times, almost as if something is pulling at her, but then she bites her lip and moves forward.

The right choice. At this moment, in this place, it doesn't matter if it's roughnecks or goblins making those sounds—if the world isn't saved from its crisis, everything is going to end.

Even so, you can't help but feel it's a shame that this might be the last image of this city that you have.

It's not as if the city is so important to you. Even your memories here barely cover an entire year. Still, you walked these streets almost every day, going to the dungeon, then you walked them almost every day going back to the inn. Those accumulated days are now on the cusp of vanishing, being taken away. It's the most natural thing in the world to mourn for them.

It's not just the city streets, either. As you pass by the Golden Knight, you see it defended by a barricade made of chairs and round tables. No doubt someone, or many someones, tried to force their way in in search of food or cash or women. There are adventurers standing under the eaves, apparently doing guard work in exchange for their tab. They watch the people passing by like hawks.

Beside them is a padfoot waitress, gripping a broom like a weapon for little reason. When the rabbit-eared woman sees you, she comes bounding over. "Are you going on an adventure?!" she asks. It seems by now she remembers you as more than just customers.

"Sure are!" Half-Elf Scout answers. "Today, we're headin' down to the very deepest depths!"

"Wow! Now, *that's* an adventure!" She claps her padded hands together audibly. Then with a perfect little smile, she gives you a great wave and exclaims, "See you, then! Be sure to stop by for a drink when you get back!" Then she adds, "We'll have everything ready for you."

You all understand what she's saying.

You give the waitress a wave in return and keep walking. Behind you, you can hear other people chatting with the waitress.

Your footsteps are light. It feels just like any other morning when you're working your way to the dungeon's entrance on the edge of town.

There she is, the royal guard standing watch.

"Hey, you're here!" she says, friendly as ever, but her face betrays how tired she is. You can't blame her. Those in charge of maintaining public safety must handle all situations at all times, and it's only natural that they need rest. They can only take that rest, though, if they have someone to back them up, to take their place. Otherwise, that rest has to be qualified: *Rest as much as possible.*

In this situation, relief from the fortress city cannot be expected, and the woman before you is the product of "as much as possible."

You tell her, sincerely, that you respect the job she's doing and ask after her younger sister.

"Thankfully, she's well." She gives you the weariest smile you've ever seen. "Just make sure you come home. Otherwise, I don't know what I'll say to her."

So that little girl is also on your side—and has great expectations. That is a grave responsibility.

"Damn straight," the royal guard says seriously. "All you adventurers are like that."

"...We'll do everything we possibly can." Female Bishop nods firmly, with much gravity.

There are some people, too clever for their own good, who say they should just send the military down there.

There are some who say there must be safer ways to make a living—as if they knew anything about it.

Others mock adventurers as fools and idiots.

You, however, do not agree.

There are some things that only adventurers can do. Things no one but an adventurer could do. Things only adventurers know. That does not change, whether they seek to earn money, to reach the top, to take revenge, or conquer the world.

That is adventure.

*What's more...*

With that in mind, you pause on the threshold of the dungeon and turn back, taking in the vista that spreads out before you. The wind comes whistling from the fortress city, bringing with it the rattling of the windmill. All the way to you.

If you should die down there in the dark, if you are setting out on your last journey, this is as good a send-off as you could wish.

As an adventurer, you cannot hope for more.

§

The darkness of the dungeon greets you as it always does, unconnected to the chaos engulfing the Four-Cornered World. You're almost nostalgic for the nervousness you felt the first time you set foot here; now, oddly, you feel practically safe.

You think you can have some sympathy for what those scruffy men living in the dungeon must have felt.

"All right...let's head for the elevator," says Female Bishop, snapping you back to reality. "Here we go."

*Mm.* You give a quick nod and then lead the party, in formation, toward the dark zone. Conversation is at a minimum; the group exchanges only necessary words. You're walking a path you went down just the other day—so why does it feel so long?

You're nervous. It's only natural. It's a bad start, you tell yourself. Worrying won't make you any more effective in battle. Of course not. How can you expect to fight at your full capacity if you behave differently from normal?

As you walk through the darkness, you wonder what you should say, how you can open a conversation.

You lose your chance when Half-Elf Scout announces, "We're here, Cap."

Just as before, you're faced with a pair of doors with a line running down the middle. You feel for the terminal, then give it a good press. The doors open.

*Let's go.* The party doesn't need your encouragement—the adventurers pile into the elevator.

You press the terminal again so that the elevator will take you to the fourth floor, down into the heart of the maelstrom, and the box begins to descend.

You feel like you're floating; like you're falling into the abyss.

You see the faces of your comrades for the first time in several hours—or maybe several minutes, or maybe several days—and to you, they look pale. Maybe it's just because of the strange magical lights that illuminate the interior of the elevator. You hope it is.

"Fwoooo...boom," Female Warrior whispers, reminding you of something she said before. You goggle at her, and she chuckles, looking back at you. "What, are you scared?"

Her face is tense despite her jibe, but you pretend not to notice; you shrug and say it's only natural.

She's trying to be thoughtful toward you, and you don't want her consideration to be in vain. Above all, you're thankful.

"Well, whatever happens down there, we're gonna be the first to know about it," Half-Elf Scout says.

This is where you would expect your cousin to chime in with something like, "Ah, so we're the tip of the spear!" But from her, you hear nothing. You search for her in the dim light inside the elevator box and find her deep in thought.

So she's thinking about something. You're smart enough to know what that means. Instead, you reply on her behalf.

*'In other words, depending how you think about it, we're the tip of the spear...'*

"Which means we can keep all the treasure for ourselves!" Half-Elf Scout exclaims, although his voice is unusually high-pitched.

"Not that we'll have much time for sightseeing," Myrmidon Monk clacks. "Not that I care either way..."

You never find out what he's going to say next. There's a heavy *thunk* and the elevator comes to a stop. The doors open.

Ahead, you see...the same thing you saw the last time. A single hallway, and beyond, a bizarre rock step that looks like some sort of altar. The design carved into the floor is dark and black, nongeometric lines running to it. An unmistakably magical glow suffuses the area, illuminating the design.

It's the center of the maze. The heart of the maelstrom.

On the floor, you see piles of ash—and weapons. Weapons that have lost their masters.

Nothing, not one thing, has changed since you withdrew from here the last time.

"...!"

Something darts in front of you: a young girl with golden hair. It's Female Bishop, who said nothing in the elevator; she's the first of you to race out, kneeling in the chamber. You hesitate over whether to call out to her and then take a step forward.

"It's okay." Female Warrior's outstretched oak spear bars your path. Her face is far less relaxed than her words; she looks fixedly at Female Bishop's back and says quietly, "Right?"

"...Yes," Female Bishop replies and nods, then gets to her feet. She takes care not to step on the piles of ash, not to tread on former friends. Leaning on the sword and scales for support, her bandaged eyes stare directly at the doors far beyond. "Because," she says, and still her voice is small, "I have to go."

You, too, look ahead. Now that you focus on it, the darkness into which the man in black vanished does somehow remind you of the elevator. Beyond the double doors, there's a coffin-like box, waiting for you.

*A casket?*

You can't resist a grim smile as the word flits through your mind. Death waits for you beyond. To enter a coffin first would be backward.

"Fwooo...boom," Female Warrior whispers in your ear.

*Third time's the charm, eh?*

Female Warrior shrugs and looks away. You pat her on the shoulder, then look around at the others and announce:

*'Let's go.'*

You stride through the doors of the elevator and look for the terminal. Four, five, six, seven, eight, and finally nine. Once you're sure everyone is on board, you punch the number for nine. And then, once more, you're falling into the abyss.

§

*All very easy to say…*

The sight that greets you as you step out on the ninth floor of the dungeon, however, is disconcertingly identical to everything else you've seen. The world, built only of shapes and shadows, shows you doors to the right and left, and a turn of the hallway up ahead. That's all. The way the place is dim, yet faintly illuminated; the aura of the unreal that pervades the hall—even the chill is the same.

It's the dungeon you know so well, the very same.

That goes some way toward calming you down.

"Thought something might jump on us the minute we got here. Guess not," mutters Myrmidon Monk from somewhere above your shoulder. Talking to himself. He has his machete in his hand, a sign of his abundant caution.

You figure this is the moment to have your scout check for enemies. You pat Half-Elf Scout on the shoulder.

"Urk! What, me?!" he says.

"That's your job, isn't it?" Female Warrior retorts with a chuckle, and your scout groans, "Gah…" A moment later, though, he steps out of the elevator.

The first tile in front of the elevator doesn't appear to sink or explode or anything. Half-Elf Scout takes a few more steps forward, silently, then he waves back to you to show it's safe.

"…Nothin' on the floor here, but there's somethin' down the way," he calls.

"What kind of something?" Female Warrior replies, readying her spear. "Is it a monster…?"

You hope you're not dealing with goblins or slimes.

Your very serious pronouncement earns you a look from Female Warrior, but she quickly faces forward again. She can tell that this isn't your usual ribbing—you really meant what you said. You want to minimize the unnecessary expenditure of energy and resources. Having two of your party members in a traumatized state is the last thing you want.

"…It's hard to believe this is really the lowest floor," Female Bishop notes, pausing in her work on the map.

"Doesn't matter. Got to keep going forward…," Myrmidon Monk says.

Of course.

You check the fastenings of your sword, then make sure everyone's got their gear before you take your first careful step onto the ninth floor. You might be in the hallway, not a chamber, but there's every chance you could encounter a wandering monster. Then there's whatever Half-Elf Scout has found—it could easily be a monster or a trap.

The lowest floor of the infamous Dungeon of the Dead lies ahead of you.

As you get closer, you can make out what Half-Elf Scout has found. It's some kind of pale thing on the wall.

And it's horrifying.

It's a woman in battered armor—but just half of her. That's the only way you can describe what you see; the other half is trapped in the wall. Her adventure ended here.

She's filthy and badly wounded, but blood still flows through her veins; you can even feel a faint warmth from her. The gentle tremors you see running through her body imply she still has breath. To your horror, you realize she is alive.

It would be bad enough if it was just the one woman, which is already terrible enough.

But she's not alone.

There are people whose arms stick out of the wall. Or just their feet. A bit of hair. Half a face.

All of them adventurers, all of them entombed within the wall.

"They—," Female Warrior starts, her voice breaking. "They're alive? These...kids?"

"...Their bodies are," replies Female Bishop in a strange tone. Yes, their bodies continue to live and breathe, but what about their hearts, their minds, their souls? How long could you last trapped alive, unable to move, all your senses cut off?

Maybe some monsters had found them and had a little fun with them, or maybe not. It's hard for you to tell.

Whatever has or has not happened, these people are embedded in the rock.

Their minds are shattered, their sparks guttering into cold ash. Their souls, you feel sure, are gone. Even if you were to break through the rock and set them free, it wouldn't change anything. You could rescue them, but you couldn't save them.

These adventurers' adventures are already over. They ended here.

"…The dimension is warped." The words come from the one member of the party who has been lost in silent thought until this moment: your cousin. "I've been thinking about it, researching it, ever since we saw that room on the fourth floor…"

She looks at the adventurers in the stone with a mix of repulsion at their pain and genuine curiosity.

It's true, you think. It's been true since you encountered the succubi. Creatures that normally exist on the dream plane can be powerful enough down here to manifest in the physical realm. You'd assumed that was simply because you were getting deeper into the dungeon— but if that altar on the fourth floor is really the dungeon's heart, then it would make sense.

You're not surprised that your cousin has gleaned some important bit of information from that.

"The rumors of Gate traps. The lost forbidden spells. But I've never heard anything about people getting trapped."

You think you hear her whisper *Of course I haven't*, but if so, it's swallowed by the emptiness and disappears.

Of course she hasn't: Anyone who ended up trapped wouldn't be around to tell the tale.

Sometimes an adventuring party disappears, leaving no sign, no trace. The rumors spread. A Gate trap. A trap sent them somewhere— but where?

*Here?*

You look at the arm stretched out in front of you, which still grasps a knife. You think it belongs to a woman. Or maybe it's a male elf— their arms might be this slender. You're not sure.

Will the adventurers who come after you think the same about you, if your party is annihilated in the dungeon?

There's no answer. These bodies are just corpses now.

"Be careful," your cousin cautions. "We don't know what might show up down here."

You nod, then steady your breathing and give your orders. If you want to advance in this ninth level, whether to find the stairs or an elevator or whatever might be out there, you'll have to move forward, go deeper in.

It's you, Female Warrior, and Half-Elf Scout up front. Your cousin, Female Bishop, and Myrmidon Monk are on the back row.

With your formation settled, the party sets out into the Dungeon of the Dead.

You proceed through the twisting hallway, kick down the farthest, deepest door you can find, and leap into the chamber.

You sense...nothing. No trace of any foes. There's only a door, leading farther on. Forward, ever forward.

You should have thought harder about what your cousin said, that the dimensional space is warped here.

You are all soon given a visceral reminder of what you've walked into.

Several giant *things* stand in the middle of the chamber.

Bluish-black, they have no skin; they look like bundles of sinews and muscle given human form.

No, no; the form isn't in imitation of humanoids. These creatures have simply found it the most effective shape for killing.

Twisted, curling horns. Massive claws. Sharp fangs. Eyes that burn in the dark. They fix you with a gaze that is utterly emotionless, except for the desire to kill.

With their horrendous odor and natural chill, these are certainly not creatures that have any right to exist in your dimension.

"Gr-greater demons...?!" The threats before you tear the scream from your cousin's lips.

This is no longer the human world.

This is dead space.

§

"GURRRRRR...!"

The massive monsters look down at you appraisingly. The light of intelligence is clear in their eyes, but it's a kind of intellect beyond human comprehension.

Demons: one of the most dangerous monsters in the Four-Cornered World, manifestations from a nonhuman plane. They even seem to live according to different laws. Mutual comprehension seems impossible.

Well, you realize, that's not quite true. There is one thing that adventurers and demons have in common: The moment they see one another, they want to kill each other.

"H-how many are there?" Female Warrior breathes.

"Can't tell!" Half-Elf Scout shouts back. "Curse 'em, drifting through the dark…!"

"Watch out—there's something else, too…!" Female Bishop calls, a salient warning not just for the front, but the back row as well. You spit on the hilt of your sword and rub it in with your palm, then you slide one foot back and face the threats in the room.

The blue-black demons look like giants to you, towering presences that signal, in your mind, the vast difference in ability between yourselves and them.

You know, of course, about greater demons. Everyone knows and fears them—although they are not as terrible as an archdemon.

If they are less terrible, though, it's not by much. In other words, they are much like adventurers: hero candidates who have not yet made their deeds known in the world, but one day might. There's no practical difference in skill between them and an archdemon. They just haven't had their opportunity yet.

Which means there's *one* thing that might provide a decisive advantage…

"They're going to call their friends, I'm sure of it!" Myrmidon Monk clacks to you from the back row. Their friends. Certainly. That would be bad. "Anyway, we need to clean them up fast or we're in trouble…!"

You respond in the affirmative at almost the same time as the enemy makes their move.

"SHUUUUUUU…!!"

That wasn't a greater demon. It's something you can't identify, striking from near the demon's feet. You slice away the monster's sharp claws with your now-unsheathed blade and bury your weapon in the creature's head. Its skull crushes inward, and you feel the soft give of brain tissue under your sword, which is now buried—in ash.

Still carried by its own momentum, the monster that attacked you turns to ash, dissolving from the head downward. Finally, it's reduced to a couple of eyeteeth that bounce toward you across the floor before they, too, are rendered ash.

*A vampire!*

"No, it hasn't reached that point yet! It's just a night stalker!" Female Bishop cries.

"Then should we use Dispel? Or should we try to seal the demons' magic? Either's good!" says Myrmidon Monk.

You shout that you'll leave it to your clerics' discretion, then throw yourself back into the battle.

"DAEMOOOOOOOONNNNN…!!"

Your job on the front row is to keep the enemy from reaching those at the back, but you're facing greater demons. They tower over you— perhaps you can nick a shin or something. The night stalkers that slither forward are a threat, but these goliaths are the real problem. You simply can't let them get past you.

One thing helps…

"Take…this!"

It's Female Warrior, wielding her oaken spear against the horde of undead, her sabbatons clicking lightly across the floor. She looks like she's dancing as she thrusts the blessed spear forward with blinding speed, stabbing one night stalker after another.

"Ha!" For the first time in a long while, you hear genuine laughter from her. "This thing is amazing!"

"Phew! Think I'll let you handle the stabbing, sister, and I'll give 'em the runaround!"

Butterfly-shaped knives flash in your scout's hands, deftly parry-ing the night stalkers' attacks. Occasionally he throws in a punch or a kick to break an enemy's form as he carves a path through the monsters.

You try to keep an eye on them, but you know you can't let your attention slip from the enemy in front of you. Holding your sword with both hands, you judge the distance, then step in when you see the moment is right, slashing with your weapon.

In a contest of sheer physical prowess, though, the demon far out-matches you.

"DEEEEEEVILLL...!!!!"

The absolute synchronicity with which the enemies from this other dimension act is itself a sort of magic, a fearsome spell.

The first thing you feel is sharp pain, like you've got cuts all over your body. The howling demon thrusts out a palm, projecting cold and ice as sharp as any blade. Balls of hail, large and small, strike you like a barrage of stones, and you can feel the chill sap the living heat from your body.

A ringing in your ears drowns out all sound; the world starts to go dark, but still you grasp your sword and refuse to let go.

For you know that your party has someone vastly accomplished in magic.

"*Musica concilio terpsichore!* Music united with dance!"

The words, half spoken, half sung, seize the greater demon's legs in a silly walk.

The Dance spell. It worked! Your cousin smiles broadly. You two are in perfect step—and you're not about to miss the opportunity she's given you.

You charge through the blizzard, which has begun to slacken, kicking hard off the ground into a leap. You fly through the air like a monkey, and you're not aiming for the creature's shin anymore.

No matter the monster, cut off its head and it will die—assuming it has a head.

With a tremendous shout you bring your katana down. Your first stroke nicks the demon's shoulder. Brackish blood spews out; as you drop, you bring the blade back up, slicing its throat.

"DAAAAAAAAAEMMMMOOONNN?!?!"

The creature gives a tremendous death roar, then crumples to the ground with an earthshaking thud. That makes one.

*But that's just a start!*

A bold claim when facing greater demons. You can't help smiling at your own finely honed skill.

"Not bad!" Female Warrior whistles, dancing another step and thrusting with her spear. Normally she aims it at the night stalkers, who come with their fangs bared like hunting dogs—but not this time. Instead she's aiming at a man in black wearing a pointed kerchief on his head—a Master Ninja! Something more powerful than the tiger-masked men you faced before; these can send a head flying with their mantis-like movements.

It's deeply unsettling to imagine such a creature sneaking up on you from the dungeon's darkness in the middle of a battle. Glad to know Female Warrior has your back as you continue your fight with the demons.

"DAEMOOOOOOONNNNN…!!!!"

The greater demons, now properly angry, thrust out their arms at you, limbs as big as trees, and the blizzard begins again. The source of that fatal cold, you heard, is in another dimension, from the river of tears in the ninth circle. That eternally frozen lake holds the evil god, the King of Terror who tried to attack the world a thousand years ago. Perhaps it's just more proof of that warped dimension…

"Hrk! Hnngh… Ah?!"

The ice nearly covers the entire room, so naturally, it reaches the back row as well. You hear Female Bishop suppress a cry just as you slash at the demon, but its sturdy muscles deflect your blade.

Were you just lucky last time? No, it was because you had your cousin's support. Your cousin, who, at this moment, is busy concentrating on her next spell. You need to buy Female Bishop time. What you must do is still the same.

Moreover, the girl isn't the helpless damsel you sometimes think of her as.

"Yah!" Female Bishop sounds almost sweet as she lashes out, but the impact that follows is anything but cute. It's the sound of the chains attached to the sword and scales groaning.

"OUURGGGRERRR?!

Despite her chattering teeth, she's forced strength into her shaking knees to deal this blow to one of the night stalkers. Blood and brains spew from the creature's shattered skull, and it turns to ash, which is quickly swept up by the blizzard and disappears.

Female Bishop brushes off the ash that's gotten on her, looking disgusted, perhaps because she can't see it.

Female Warrior, pulling her spear out of the ninja, turns back long enough to shout, "I'm sorry! One of them got past me!"

"It's okay! Don't blame yourself!" Female Bishop says. Three people alone in the front row isn't quite enough to deal with all these enemies. One of them was bound to slip by.

You give everyone their orders, saying that you'll continue to deal with the demons, and then you level your blade once more at the massive form before you. Even though the collection of sinew is bleeding otherworldly blue-black blood, the blizzard continues at full intensity.

Surely even the demon can be distracted. That's all you need. You aren't fighting alone.

*"Sword-prince, to those who see what should be seen and speak what should be spoken, grant your protection!"*

*There, see!*

Female Bishop's prayer, chanted with lips turning blue, reaches the gods in heaven and saves your life. A curtain of divine protection falls between you and the cold, and you force strength into your numb fingers, finding your mark.

Once, twice. Again and again. Your blade dances toward the massive arm, wounding it. You don't need a critical hit like you got earlier. Even grazing wounds will shave away the monster's pile of hit points and help open that crucial opportunity.

"We need to deploy some healing!" your cousin shouts.

"No, first we have to stop them from casting any more spells! If they get off a second blast, we may be done for!" Female Bishop says.

"I'll coordinate with you! If we can cut off their spell casting, the demons ought to weaken!" says Myrmidon Monk.

"All right, let's do it!"

It doesn't have to be you who creates that window. If it did, why would you even have a party?

As you and the others on the front row put everything on the line to hold the enemies at bay, those in the back are fighting a desperate struggle of their own.

*"My god the roaming wind, let all we say on the road stay secret among us!"*

*"Let the light of quietude be upon you!"*

A pure wind and a holy flare like the light of the sun fill the chamber, much to the demons' astonishment. These creatures work magic as readily as they breathe, and taking that power from them is not easy. Even you, who can speak a few words of true power, understand that it's more difficult than you can imagine.

The two clerics in your party make it look easy.

Nor are they your only two companions.

"____?!"

"Yesss! You're mine!" With an almost joyous shout, a colorful wind rushes across the floor. The blades in Half-Elf Scout's hands are bright as butterfly wings. You hear them ring out, and in the time it takes you to blink twice, a meteor with a tail of blue blood is stretching out before you.

The two demons in front of you abruptly tilt forward. The tendons of their legs are severed—just as you originally planned.

"Took you long enough!"

Female Warrior has been waiting for this moment, and she leaps, her body taut as a bowstring. Have the stolen magic and crumpled bodies of the demons bought you enough time to admire her beauty?

The oaken spear whistles through the air as if to mock the silenced demons. It lands a critical hit, piercing one through the heart.

"___?! ____?!"

"Ha-ha-ha! What's that? I can't hear you!" Female Warrior yells, laughing. The fountain of blue-black blood from the monster fails to reach her where she stands smirking.

She plants her sabbaton on the monster's chest, kicking off and propelling herself backward. The creature collapses as if the kick is the last straw.

One left.

Losing no time, you slide toward the last demon, closing in on it. Your earlier flurry of attacks and the bevy of wounds they inflicted have not been in vain. You were targeting its tissues—alter-planar demon or no, it's still made of flesh and bone.

Letting your faithful blade lead you, you raise your sword, lifting it easily. You step in, and it rises like the sparks of a campfire blown by the wind. You place your other hand on the hilt and flip it around.

You take another step, letting your reversed blade ride its own momentum downward.

*Shmp.* You remember the feel under your hands, like slicing a straw training post. Both of the demon's arms are severed at the elbow.

You spot your next target and draw back your sword, which slices flesh and bone.

"____?!"

The demon gives a great, voiceless cry and waves its useless arms. It looks almost silly flailing around, except that its tremendous size makes even this unfocused violence dangerous. You get some distance to make sure one of the arms doesn't smash you or break your leg, and vigilantly stand with your sword at the ready.

You don't expect an intelligent monster like a demon to behave like a creature with no intellect. It must be doing something. But what?

Female Bishop's head jerks up; something has tipped off her sharp intuition. She shouts, "It's trying to call more of them!"

You have no reason, no reason at all, to doubt her judgment. You know only two clerics as powerful as she is, and only two spell casters. One of them, Myrmidon Monk, clacks his mandibles and watches closely; your cousin brings up her short staff, her expression serious.

*Warped space, huh?*

It's not intuitive to you—but if that thing calls its friends from another dimension, you'll be in real trouble.

"What do we do? Do we finish it here and now or hunt a bit after there are more of them? I don't care either way!"

"I don't think the more's the merrier in this case—just go for it!" Half-Elf Scout yells.

*Let's do it!* Your judgment is swift, and your cousin's response is even swifter. As the one responsible for overseeing your party's resources, she raises her staff high and shouts, "Coordinate with me!"

"Right!" Female Bishop responds, raising the sword and scales. This will be her third consecutive spell. You're burning through your magic at an alarming rate.

You glance at your cousin. She nods. Without hesitation, you raise your hand and weave a spell.

The words of true power that you, her, and Female Bishop incant are but three:

*"Ventus!"*

*"Lumen!"*

'Libero!'

Run free, wind and light!

The next instant, a whirlwind fills the chamber along with a flash of light and heat. This is the overwhelming power one can draw from the Demon Core. Perhaps the only thing that could withstand this power that lies at the root of all things is the black-scaled storm bringer the lizardmen speak of in their myths.

No demon, no night stalker, no monster that lurks in the dark can hope to prevail against it.

As ice melts, so the monsters turn to dust, unable even to scream, and are lost.

All that remains is enough heat to make your skin prickle, drifting back to you on the wind. The only sign that there were ever any monsters in this chamber is the treasure chest that has appeared as if from nowhere.

You don't let down your guard until the last moaning of the explosion has left your ears. The silence that remains is almost painful, and it is then that you finally let out a breath.

You shake the blood off your blade and check how your friends are doing, your usual custom.

"Huh! Shows what a greater demon is worth," Half-Elf Scout jokes.

He turns toward the chest, and Female Warrior laughs. "Yeah! Without their spells, all they can do is outnumber us." She smiles like a cat and brushes her black hair back. Maybe she's trying to look a little stronger than she feels, but she's making no attempt to hide her injuries. It's a way of bringing her back to herself, to get her feet back under her. There's no problem with that.

"How far have we come? I'd like to see the map," your cousin says.

"Oh, certainly. I'm still working on it… Give me a second."

Your cousin is paying close attention to how Female Bishop looks. You couldn't be more grateful.

Female Bishop opens her bag and grabs the parchment roll she'd stuffed

©lack

away, taking out her scrawled notes. You're impressed: She sketches out the geography of the room you've entered, completely by feel.

"Two up, two across… Hmm…"

"There might be a hidden door. I'll look later," says Myrmidon Monk from over her head.

"Yes, please." Female Bishop nods like a baby bird. "I'll have to prepare Holy Light…"

She sounds just a little bit…eager.

You know that she used three separate spells in the fight just now, though.

Your cousin mutters "Hrmm" at about the same moment Female Bishop finishes her work.

"Here you go. I think we're about in the middle of the ninth floor."

"Thanks!" your cousin says, taking the map Female Bishop offers her and trotting over to you.

You're at the halfway point—and yet the exploration has just begun.

Your cousin offers the map to you happily, and about as you expected, only the lower right corner is filled in. Thinking back on the other levels of the dungeon you've experienced, though, barely half of them proceed directly ahead, or "upward."

What does she think? Notwithstanding her smug look, your cousin's eyes are serious. So you make a point of sighing and saying something about how it's stuff like this that makes your *second* cousin drive you up the wall.

She makes an obliging show of getting angry: "You know I'm older than you, right?! I'm like your big sister!" You grin, then jerk your chin toward Female Bishop. She's by the wall, her hands to her modest chest in a gesture of relief. You can see her exhale; you can hear the "Phew" from where you're standing, although you can't hear whatever she says after that. You think she looks a bit tired.

*'Might be wise to take a short rest.'*

"I agree," your *second* cousin says, nodding grimly. "That was some battle."

It's all too rare that you're given a moment like this so far down in the dungeon. You pull holy water from your bag and pour it in a circle around yourselves.

That's when you hear it.

*Ka-clank. Ka-clank.*

The sound of something metal slapping against the ground, coming toward you from down the hall.

§

It almost sounds like one of the strange and silly musical instruments that jesters play. The source of the noise is nearly as strange—it is, indeed, a bizarre animal. The clanking turns out to come from a massive steel box that wanders into view.

It drags itself along on feet that look like accordion bellows, producing a noise like something scraping against a knight's armor. At first glance it looks like a wagon or a chariot, perhaps, but there certainly aren't any horses attached to it.

If it's wandering the dungeon, one thing's for sure: It's a living, moving monster.

"What," says Half-Elf Scout, his voice breaking, "is *that?*"

As surprised as you all were by the creature's appearance, you also reacted quickly, crouching in a corner of the chamber and trying not to breathe. You've just come out of a major battle; it's the worst possible time to be ambushed by something you can't even identify. That was what motivated your choice of action, and it wasn't a mistake.

You feel the same way as your scout. *What* is *it?*

"I have no idea…," Female Bishop whispers back, her voice high and trembling with fear. Her senses can tell her that whatever is approaching is threatening, but she can't deduce much more than that. "There's nothing I can say…"

You see how frightened she is, and you assure her with no trace of humor that it's not a goblin.

Female Bishop smiles oh so slightly, although her face is still tense. "Right," she says, nodding. That's a good start.

"You've been reading a lot of books lately. Have you seen anything about that?" Myrmidon Monk asks your cousin.

"Unfortunately, only demons know much about the biology of demons," she replies. Those spell books from strange lands that she's been so assiduous in collecting and studying contain information about a great many things—so how about man-eating fiends? Maybe, maybe not, but even your cousin's expertise isn't helping here.

*'No, wait. What did you say just now?'*

"Only, uh... Oh!" She nods at you. "That it's a demon."

*Good gods.* You groan to yourself, then place a hand on your sword, so recently returned to its scabbard. You'd assumed it wasn't a creature of this world—so bizarre monsters like that can also be found in demons' lairs.

"What do we do? Do we take it?" Myrmidon Monk clacks at you, as nonchalant as ever. He doesn't care either way.

"...Hmm. I'm not sure there's any need to fight," Female Warrior whispers seductively in your ear; you can hear her tinkling laugh right next to you.

You find yourself remembering your encounter with the succubi. Why? No, this is different.

You glance to the side. There's no hint of fear on Female Warrior's face, only her usual catlike expression.

"After all, we're going to the deepest level of the dungeon, aren't we? I don't think we should fight when we don't have to."

You can't quite decide if it's conscious or intuitive for her, but that tone, that expression—they're the way she always is. You're grateful for it. A group that has only one opinion is a dangerous thing, of course.

You cross your arms, ponder, and watch the steel demon as it wanders around, making its unearthly noise. You wonder how it can even tell where it's going.

Half-Elf Scout likewise crosses his arms and mutters, "Well now... Think it's got eyes? Or ears?" Even he, now an accomplished scout, has to pause and consider how to evade a completely unknown monster. "It's hardly even got a head."

"Maybe it uses smell!" your cousin says.

"Naw, it woulda found us all long ago," Half-Elf Scout replies, but then he laughs and says, "Clever girl." He nods. "Point is, it can't seem to find us where we're hiding. Doesn't mean we can let our guard down, though."

Makes sense. You express your gratitude for your scout's analysis, and then continue carefully watching the creature. It's probably pointless to wonder what it's thinking, given that it comes from a completely different dimension.

It shambles around the chamber. There's an enemy in the room, and you don't know how it will act…

Silently you reach for your sheaths and draw the short blade that's been waiting.

"What? Think you can hit a vital point?" A chuckle follows that question; it's Female Warrior, who's looking over your shoulder.

*Hardly.* A ghost of a smile plays on your lips. You do wish, however, that you'd learned better how to fight with a knife—much better for close quarters like this.

You grab the knife like you're a particularly wild member of the family Felidae, then aim in an entirely unexpected direction and fling it. The small blade pierces through the darkness, bouncing off the wire frame in the distance.

The steel demon reacts instantaneously. It turns what you take to be its head, and the horn growing there lashes out.

No, you realize, it's not a horn; that was your mistake. It seems to be more of a magic staff.

There's an explosive *boom*, and then a geyser of flame.

"_____?!"

Female Warrior claps her hands over her ears at the deafening sound and shouts something you can't hear over the blast. The noise echoes inside your helmet. Scrunching up your face and crouching down is the most you can do. The rest of your party is in much the same position; only Myrmidon Monk seems largely unaffected. The successive explosions simply cause his feelers to bounce a little. You're sort of jealous.

"I guess this goes beyond simple fire breath," he clacks.

"Wh-what…did you say?" your cousin asks, shaking her head vigorously. She probably literally couldn't hear him.

You groan amidst the vaporized debris drifting through the air from the steel demon's attack. Somehow, even though you can't hear anything, there's a high-pitched ringing in your ears. You just can't win with this thing!

"That was probably a magical blast," says Myrmidon Monk, who's managed to "purse" his antennae in a way that looks almost as frustrated as your groaning. "Might be poison, might be paralysis... maybe even petrification. Point is, we would be facing a hail of those things."

"Basically, take one of those hits and it's game over, huh?" Half-Elf Scout asks with a shrug. You sympathize.

So this creature uses sound and perhaps its eyes (although you don't know what it can see).

"Magic blasts, strange sounds, breath weapon, strange footsteps..." Female Bishop seems to be onto something where you aren't. Maybe it helps that she doesn't have sight to distract her. She's placed a slim finger to her lips and is thinking. At length, she says, "Maybe it's... Hell's Jester!"

"You know, now that you mention it...!" Your cousin claps her hands and nods, but you, meanwhile, don't know what they mean. You ask if there's really a demon with a name like that, and your cousin replies, "Well, there aren't a lot of records. The book I saw only called it an unidentified demon who supposedly approached with a sound like a jester's lute."

If you've now encountered such a creature yourself, that's of immense academic interest—but you're not editors of the *Monster Manual*. At this moment, you need to know just one thing: how you can kill it.

"Hmm... Well, like I said, not many people have seen one, and even fewer have written about it." Your cousin scrunches up her face, deep in thought, and you wait for her to answer, unhurried. You're pleased even just to learn that this creature isn't completely unknown; you're glad to have identified it. It means someone, somewhere, survived an encounter with this monster.

If there's data available, perhaps it can even be killed.

After a few moments of furrowing her eyebrows and rubbing her temples, your cousin turns to you and says without much confidence,

"Some people say the exterior is just a façade, that the tongue is the true body, or that maybe there's a slime inside…?"

"Urgh…" Female Warrior scowls. Or maybe she looks like she's about to cry. Whichever it is, the sound she makes is pitiful.

You pat her on the back with a grin, then conclude that the point is, if you can get that thing's armor off, you might be able to do something about it. It's not realistic to think you could dodge past those terrible magic blasts only to spend the rest of your time in the dungeon with the fear you might encounter this thing again. It's clear what you must do if you want to get to the tenth floor.

*We have to hit that steel demon and smash it.*

"Basically, we gotta do something about that pesky flack it's got," Half-Elf Scout comments. He watches the monster, which ambles around at an irregular pace.

No, you realize: What he's studying is the chamber that's set to be the stage for your battle.

You whisper that you wish there were some way to draw first blood. You need to get that armor or shell or whatever it is off that thing or you have no hope here. You don't think frying it (or would that be steaming it?) in its armor is very likely.

In which case, you're going to need an obstacle. You don't think a frontal assault with sword and spear would get you very far.

"Those magical blasts, those are the problem. I'm not sure even Protection could stop them." Female Bishop sounds surprisingly engaged, though; if the party asked, she would no doubt use her miracle.

Half-Elf Scout blinks at that, then jerks his thumb toward the room. "We've got what we need. Barriers."

"Wha…?" Of course Female Bishop can't tell what he's pointing out right away; she can't see it.

You have the thing the party is hiding behind at this moment. Then the walls that make up the chamber. Half-Elf Scout is pointing at something between them. The corpses of the greater demons, as big as you could want.

§

An explosion sounds, smoke billows up. The shock and the heat ride the air toward you, and you run to meet them. Each time a round explodes over your head, the demon's corpse bounces, bits of flesh flying off it.

"Ugh, greater demon innards!" cries Female Warrior as some viscera come down on top of her. It's still better than taking a direct hit.

Nonetheless, the blasts fired by the steel demon, the jester of hell, remain formidable. Its shots easily strip away the exterior of the demons against whom you struggled so mightily.

*Huh! That diamond knight acted like he was going to have the tougher time, going to the capital!*

Is there any greater adventure than braving the depths of the Dungeon of the Dead? And you're only on the ninth floor.

In spite of it all, the great, thick walls of meat have proven more than enough to withstand the monster's breath. You've tucked yourself behind the corpse; now Female Warrior runs to join you, her breath coming in ragged gasps. Then you both crouch behind the body.

There's another blast, and another demon-shaking shockwave.

"What are we supposed to do about *that*...?" You decide the whine in Female Warrior's voice must be due to the blue-black body fluids she's soaked in. You'll have to lend her a handkerchief later, you think, but for now you say that's a good question and start thinking seriously.

That thing has a shell like a suit of armor. No ordinary blow is going to reach it.

Normally, then, you'd look for a chink in the armor. On any decent suit of plate mail, the joints would be covered, but that thing is an altar-planar monster. You need to let Female Bishop rest, however, and you want to conserve your other spells if you can.

You decide a strategy like the one you used on the green dragon is called for.

"You've got it... Hee-hee." The laughter seems to come unbidden to Female Warrior's lips; she doesn't appear to expect it, and you certainly don't. You look at her in shock, to find yourself meeting her translucent eyes. "Nothing," she says, shaking her head, her black hair rippling. "This is just sort of...fun."

That's all. Leaving behind only that brief whisper and the sweet scent of her hair, she pushes off the ground with her sabbatons and rushes off. Left on your own, you watch in astonishment as she goes—and then you laugh.

Yes, this is what you're cut out for. What you must do hasn't changed. You'll brave the deepest depths of the Dungeon of the Dead. That's what this adventure is about. You wouldn't trade it with the Knight of Diamonds for anything. Maybe he's struggling away in the capital right now, or maybe he's taking on the forces of evil at the head of a great army. Whichever it is, you wish he could see you now. He'll regret his choice later on.

"Yo, Cap! What do we do about this?" Half-Elf Scout shouts in between bursts. Sneaking is his specialty, but you don't see any shadows anywhere. As for the shouting, he probably figures that with all the explosions going on, the enemy won't hear him over its own attacks.

Every bit as loud as the magical explosions, you shout back that you're going to give it the runaround; then you press your helmet against the demon's rapidly disintegrating flesh.

You can't see the faces of your back row from where you are—but you figure they're okay. Your cousin and Myrmidon Monk are there. They'll keep an eye on Female Bishop lest she bites off more than she can chew.

Anyway—yes, this is still the ninth floor. Just the ninth floor. The tenth level, and the man in black, still await. Right now, conserving your energy is even more important to you than getting Female Bishop rest.

At that point in your thinking, another smile creeps onto your face. Sparing a thought for the back row? Seems like you're as relaxed as anything.

Yes... *Yes, this is better by far.*

With a remarkably light heart, you grip your katana and leap out from behind the demon's corpse.

"_____!"

The steel demon turns to look at you and makes some sort of vocalization; the horn—no, the staff—spewing magic begins to change trajectory. This creature seems to be able to rotate its head in a complete circle, but the magic attack can only come from its staff. At least that means that if you attack from three different directions, you can't all be wiped out at once.

"—!!"

There's an earsplitting screech of metal and the "boom stick," the staff growing from the creature's head, explodes like a high tower.

You immediately jump back—yeah, right.

More like you'll be blown back when something hits you—the light, the sound, one of them. So you have to stay one step ahead. Any time the opponent moves, you have to move first. Keep going. That's all you can do.

The tongues of fire get close enough to lick you; you roll to avoid them. What must you look like to those watching from the back row? Your cousin is probably anxious, but maybe not Female Bishop—since she can't see you. As for Myrmidon Monk...

*Get hit, don't get hit... He probably doesn't care either way.*

*Sounds about right.* Such are the silly thoughts that pass through your mind as you plant a palm on the floor of the chamber and heft yourself up. There's no time to stand still. That would simply give the enemy a chance to target you. That's the last thing you want. Instead, you bounce like a ball with your sword at the ready, running, always running.

It's not like you're simply fleeing in a panic. The enemy is locked on to you now, and as far as it goes, you're grateful for that.

"Hey! How d'ya like *this*?!"

While the monster is busy going after you, Half-Elf Scout lunges at it, bringing his butterfly-shaped knives to bear on its feet. They're strange and bellows-like, but they're still feet. The muscles are easily severed, and the torso lists to one side.

The feet suddenly start to scramble along the floor, making an awful screech—but also providing a critical opening; one that Female Warrior isn't about to miss.

"——?!"

Female Warrior shouts "Yaaah!" and leaps through the air, even her sabbatons barely clicking as she threads her way among the magical fire. The spear in her hand shines with an almost divine light, even down here in the darkness. She drives it into the monster's shell.

"_____?!?!?!"

"Ha!" says Female Warrior, licking her lips. "So we *can* hurt you!"

She leans her weight against her weapon, and even though she's not a very big person, the spear acts like a lever, prying at the creature's shell. There's a creaking, then a cracking, the noise somewhere between steel shattering and flesh tearing. The one thing that's very clear is that the steel demon is in intense pain.

And so you run.

You push off from the floor of the chamber, and then, using the greater demon's corpse as a ramp—you leap.

Your armor weighs heavy on your legs, the strain of continuous battle weighs heavy on your body, but the flying monkey technique that your master taught you is stronger than them both.

As you fly through the air, you form a sigil with your left hand, your lips speaking words of true power.

Just three words, to be precise.

*Carbunculus Crescunt Iacta.*

A ball of ethereal fire flies from your fingertips, trailing a tail of spectral light as it drops squarely into the monster's open wound.

Whereupon...

"?!?!?!?!?!?!?!!!??!?!"

There's a muffled *thump* from the creature's stomach, then black smoke begins pouring out of its body.

"Ahhh!"

That's not the reason for Female Warrior's scream, however. She screams because something a dark crimson color has come flying out of the smoking monster. It's an engorged slime—no, it writhes like the tongue of some unknown creature.

It jumped right at Female Warrior's head, which was when she screamed and crouched down so that the tongue went flying over her.

"No! It's gonna get away...!" Half-Elf Scout hollers.

You may not know exactly what it is, but what it's trying to do is obvious. You turn at Half-Elf Scout's warning, but the room is large and the distance is great. The monster's tongue squirms its way across the floor, making a lunge for the hallway.

"*Aranea facio ligator!* Spider, come and bind!"

Formed by the very rhythm of the incantation, a sticky white substance ensnares the tongue and drags it to the ground.

"It's hard to cast spells directly on demons, but indirect magic works just fine!" your cousin says with a triumphant snort. Her staff is thrust out, much like her ample chest.

No, wait—she's actually standing tall to protect Female Bishop behind her.

*An admirable performance indeed.*

…is what you don't say to her.

Nonetheless, your relief must be written on your face. Your cousin chuckles, pleased with herself.

"Well, whatever it is," Myrmidon Monk clacks, looking down at the writhing tongue in the spiderweb with no pity in his compound eyes, "this is the end of it, right?"

Then he gives it a good whack with his machete—and indeed, that ends things.

§

It's only natural to take a short rest after that. You draw a circle with holy water to keep monsters at bay, then each of you finds a place for yourself, relaxing in whatever manner you choose. You might be in the dungeon, you might be right in the middle of a chamber, but uninterrupted exploring is not a good idea. This is necessary.

*How many times is it now—stopping for a rest in the dungeon like this?*

What happened the first time you visited the first floor? You think about it, about how many times you've braved these depths since then. Over and over.

You mull the thought as you head to the corner where Half-Elf Scout is crouched. He's positioned himself in front of the treasure chest that appeared as if from nowhere, working with his seven tools to break the lock. He told you to keep your distance—this is dangerous business, after all—but it's SOP for you to station yourself nearby while he works.

"What, wonderin' if we're gonna find ourselves a magic weapon down here?" Half-Elf Scout asks, sparing you a glance as you come up beside him. "With our luck, we'll get holy armor or a paladin's cloak or something. Lotta good that'll do us."

But if you live to go home, you could sell it for a nice price.

"True enough," Half-Elf Scout responds with a laugh.

Those particular items might not be of use to your party, but there's always a chance that a magic sword might appear.

This time your words are half-serious. "Also true." The scout nods, then adds almost in a whisper, "Hell, this is like a dream."

*Hoh*, you breathe. How unusual, for him to give you any hint of his inner life. He's always considerate of the other party members, always trying to do things for them.

You cross your arms and lean against the wall, indicating that you're listening to your scout. If he wants to talk, he can talk. To listen is your job; at least, that's what you think.

"Me, I was just a penniless scout," he says. "A washed-up adventurer, or at least getting there."

One wrong move and he would have been just a runner, he says, as his tools rattle in the lock.

You're more than familiar with this scout's skill by now—he would have made a very good runner.

"Naw, can't think that way. I joined a party 'cause I felt like I had to, but it all sorta went to hell."

He shrugs, a half grin on his face. There's another rattle from the lock.

That must've been when he pissed off the wizard and wound up in a tree—you laugh, remembering how the two of you met. Maybe he stole that spell book and maybe he didn't, but whatever, he ended up with a spell of bug attraction on him, up in a tree and hounded by bees.

You and your cousin were passing by on your way to the fortress city when he begged you for help.

"And now the likes of me is on the deepest floor of the Dungeon of the Dead. Wouldn't believe it if I hadn't been there."

You remind him that you all might still die before you get there. "Oof!" He groans and looks at the ceiling.

There's one more metallic scrape, and then the lid of the chest pops open, revealing what's inside: money, treasure, equipment. A pretty good take.

©lack

"Gotta get back alive so we can see exactly what we have here," Half-Elf Scout says softly with a glance in Female Bishop's direction. You nod and pat him on the shoulder. One more reason, you suggest, that you need to send that guy's head flying.

"Wouldn't get my hopes up if I were you," Half-Elf Scout warns with a grin that shows his teeth. It makes you think of a shark.

You leave him to collect the loot in a sack while you sit down to get a little rest yourself.

*We...*

You sink into thought. We, your party, were not chosen by the gods, not burdened with some destiny. Female Warrior's oaken spear is blessed, yes, but it would be absurd to take that as evidence that either of you has been divinely chosen. It was, after all, the nun of the Trade God who blessed the spear, and to borrow her words, it is all things and everything that support the formed and formless alike. To be connected to that doesn't mean anything special about you.

You're just adventurers. Not different from anyone else. The moment you arrived at the fortress city, you were:

Just a warrior.

His cousin.

A wrung-out scout.

A girl raised to become a hero.

A young woman sold off to pay her taxes.

A monk from a foreign land who keeps his own faith.

That's all.

The six of you are no more than that, yet here you are, standing on the ninth floor of the dungeon.

Fearing goblins, fearing slimes, tussling with bushwhackers, all but decapitated by a ninja, fighting with other adventurers. Now you stand on the very doorstep of the man in black who rules over the Dungeon of the Dead.

It is a strange and wonderful thing.

In your mind, the danger facing the world never meant that much, yet here you are.

*Feel sorry for the diamond knight. Oh well.*

You get just a few winks of shut-eye, cradling your sword. As the thoughts pass through your mind, you smile.

§

*Think it's time to get going.*

It's a bit later.

You stand up, tighten the fasteners on your armor, and call out to your party. Your sense of time is hazy, but you think the Knight of Diamonds and his group must be getting started about now.

You check the state of your blade, make sure the handle is firm, and then slide it into its scabbard with an audible *click*.

The miasma in the dungeon is familiar by now, the cold stone and oppressive wire frame like old friends. The very fact that you can relax at all down here could be considered proof of how experienced you are.

The same is true of the rest of your party. They've been sitting and taking a break, but at your words they stand up and start to get ready.

"Are you going to be all right?" your cousin asks, going over to Female Bishop, who seems somewhat out of it.

"…Yes," she says after a second. "I'm fine."

"Well, if you need anything, just tell me. *He* wouldn't know how to be nice to a girl if his life depended on it!"

*Yeah, sure.* Second *cousin.* This offhanded dismissal is all you offer to her barbed remark before you turn to Myrmidon Monk and ask him how he's doing. You want to get everyone's perspective before the party moves out.

"Well, whatever, we have to decide whether to go forward or head back. Haven't gone *too* far from the elevator yet."

He unfurls the map with a flutter. He must have borrowed it from Female Bishop while they were resting. This myrmidon is your party's most skilled cartographer.

Myrmidon Monk runs a sharp claw along the map, tapping your current location. "Distance-wise, we're right in the middle. Go on to the tenth floor, or go back. I don't care either way."

"We've been pretty conservative with our spells, so at least we've got some leeway there," Half-Elf Scout pipes up from beside you, peeking at the map. He's not a spell user himself; it's your cousin who's responsible for managing the party's resources. As such, if he's saying something so reasonable, it must be in large part a show of consideration to the others. "Stamina's another thing, though. Won't do us any good to get down there wheezing and bloodied."

"What, tired already?" Female Warrior coos, smiling her catlike smile. By this point, you know what's behind this act. You glance at her, and she winks at you coquettishly. "Well, that won't do. Girls don't like a guy who *gets tired* too easily." She nudges Half-Elf Scout with the butt of her spear.

"Aw, shaddup," the scout shoots back.

Female Warrior makes sure to strike the coup de grâce by calling back to Female Bishop, "Am I wrong?"

The two of them are often at the temple together. They became fast friends practically before you noticed. The thought would bring a smile to your face—but you're too busy asking Female Bishop what she thinks of the situation.

"Wha—?" She looks at you, surprised to be the focus of attention. "Um, well..." She seems hesitant, unsure, and isn't able to answer immediately. You don't get annoyed at her but simply wait for her to collect herself.

You think this is only natural. If someone called on you the same way, you wouldn't simply instinctively agree. The six of you are all different people. You have different thoughts, different origins, different classes—everything about you is different.

"If you ask me... I think we may not get another chance," she says.

That's why you need to hear what Female Bishop thinks. Her experience of adventure to this point has enabled her to give confident voice to her feelings.

"I want to put an end to this," she adds.

You feel sure that it's the strength that has been inside her from the very beginning. It had simply been obscured by all the stuff that had piled up on top of it. You're genuinely happy to see it emerge again.

*Then let's go.*

Thus, as clearly as Female Bishop, you render your decision.

The members of the party look at each other, and then, as one, they nod.

Myrmidon Monk: "Go straight to settle this with the Big Bad? Sounds interesting. Count me in."

Half-Elf Scout: "Heh-heh-heh-heh! Even a Demon Lord would be child's play for me!"

Female Warrior: "Well, well. Sounds like if we lose this fight, we know who to blame."

"Oof…" (The scout again.)

"We'll be just fine. I'm counting out all of you!" your cousin says. Very in character, but you're going to need her to help out, too. So you inform her of this with a bit of a smile, and then you set out at a slow trot for the depths of the dungeon.

You have no way of knowing what awaits you.

*No…*

In one way, you know exactly what's waiting. Monsters, loot, the maze—and beyond, the man in black.

No different from everything else you've experienced down here. Meaning that what you must do hasn't changed, either.

You don't know how many of you will survive. You don't know how badly this fight may injure you.

*But…*

What do you care?

Harboring no doubts, you press forward. All of you, together.

*That's what it means to be an adventurer.*

The way to the tenth floor is not a staircase, but a hole, one that leads into the abyss.

You stand at the farthest extremity of the ninth floor and peer into it, into a darkness that seems to lead to the very bowels of the earth.

*There's no wind.*

You didn't expect to be able to see anything in the blackness, but there isn't even the breath of a breeze coming up from the depths.

This does not feel like a place people should tread—but it's awfully late to be worrying about that.

*This was surprisingly close to the elevator.* You mutter, purposely, that you ended up taking quite a detour.

"Whoever built this maze was rotten to the core, I tell ya," Half-Elf Scout says, picking up the thread with a theatrical shake of his head.

Female Bishop giggles. "Unlike on the fourth and fifth floor, it doesn't seem like there are any hidden areas down here."

After this calm assessment, she brushes a hand along the dungeon wall. The one packed full of trapped adventurers, bristling with arms and legs and other body parts in a wretched array. There can't possibly be some secret hidden within it. It's merely an adventurers' graveyard.

"Which makes me think…if we want to get to the tenth floor, this is the only way to do it," Female Bishop says.

"Gives me the creeps…," Female Warrior grumbles, frowning

openly. She taps the edge of the pit with the butt of her spear and looks at you. "How do we know it's not just full of spikes at the bottom?"

Maybe she's needling you, maybe she's worried—or maybe both. You tell her you figure it will work out somehow, as you peer into the hole.

"If they wanted to set a trap, I think they would have picked somewhere more traditional," Myrmidon Monk says, his antennae bobbing. He offers that he thinks there's a bottom to this pit. "What bothers me more is that there doesn't seem to be a way to get back out."

"I don't think we have to worry about that," says your cousin, who nonetheless looks nonplussed as she looks into the pit. You move around behind her, ready to grab her collar at any time if she should get too close and start to fall. You're not sure what she's thinking. "I mean, think about it. *He* managed to come up here."

The man in black. Now that she mentions it, that's true. If he can come and go at will, then there must be some way to get down to the tenth floor, and some way to get back up.

At the very least…you pick up what your cousin is saying, thinking about the sight of the sun as you do.

*At the very least, we should be on the right track—he took the elevator himself.*

Meaning that this floor, this area, should offer some way down to the bottom level.

A giant, yawning hole, perhaps.

"That's assuming this isn't a clever trap he set because he knows we'll think that," Female Warrior snaps. You're actually grateful for it. Vigilance, suspicion, and even cowardice are all necessary things.

You nod, then jerk your chin in the direction of Half-Elf Scout and Female Bishop; one of them the most perceptive member of your party, the other not distracted by what she sees. Not even Myrmidon Monk and his antennae can quite match them.

"……I do feel something. A strange aura," Female Bishop begins haltingly after listening closely to the hole. "If it was just a bottomless pit, I don't…I don't think it would feel like this."

"The thing about a trap is, ya usually try to *hide* it," quips Half-Elf

Scout, carefully surveying every inch of the rim of the hole and finally standing up.

There was one spot with a door that wouldn't open; when it was pried open, on the other side was a wall. That would seem to imply that this pit is the only path left.

"Gotta wonder if our rope is long enough to get us down there...," says Half-Elf Scout.

"I know the Slow Down spell—that should let us down gently," replies your cousin. With that, the final problem is solved. Meaning...

"Meaning today is the day that fool dies," Myrmidon Monk clacks out. "Very interesting."

Lastly, you take a look around at your party. Everyone looks squarely back at you. Your feelings, and your answer, are united.

*The tenth floor, eh?*

With this appreciative murmur, you tell your cousin you're counting on her, and then you throw yourself into the darkness, into the abyss.

"*Terra...semel...levius!* Earth, for a time, grow lighter!"

Your cousin's words of true power follow you down—still it feels like they take an eternity.

"Just don't look up, okay?" Female Warrior jokes.

You hear the others come after you, one by one. "Eek!" cries one of the girls—Female Bishop or your cousin, you can't be sure.

*One thing's clear: Whatever happens, this won't be boring.*

§

"...Huh! Looks about the same as everything else," Half-Elf Scout says, and he's exactly right.

You land in a dark, cramped, and very familiar dungeon hallway. You still see nothing but wire frame. The only appreciable difference is a stone stela standing in front of you. It bears a gold plaque inscribed with words in an ancient language:

FOR YOU—DEATH.

The Dungeon of the Dead.

Yes, that's what this is, why it bears that name.

You look in each direction, trying to decide which way to go. You're about to set foot into the darkness when—

"Be careful!" your cousin shouts, and you freeze.

Slowly, you bring your foot back to where it was and turn around. Your cousin's face is pale and bloodless.

"This space is warped. Even worse than on the ninth floor…" She hugs herself and shudders as if from cold, then she looks up at you and says hoarsely, "If we aren't careful where we step, who knows where we might find ourselves…?"

"Well, how are we supposed to walk *anywhere* like that?" Female Warrior says, a tremble in her voice as if she might start crying at any moment. "I don't want to end up like…*them*…"

You know what she must be thinking of: the adventurers buried in the wall on the ninth floor. Nobody would want to end up condemned to spend all eternity as a plaything, providing "comfort" to the dungeon's inhabitants.

You pat her on the shoulder in an attempt to calm her down and ask your cousin if it's at all possible to see the distortions.

She looks very thoughtful for a moment, chewing on her thumbnail and staring into space. "I almost feel like it's…sort of like a whirlpool…"

It's Female Bishop who finally provides the real answer. "To the left, I think." She stretches a long, slim finger, pointing down the left branch of the hallway. "It's sort of…" She makes a spinning motion in the air with one hand. "It's like the flow of the whirlpool goes from left to right. That's what it feels like to me. So…"

So going to the left would take you toward the center of the whirlpool, the center of the distortion. As for what you'll find there—that's clear enough.

*The man in black.*

"That settles it, then." The clacking of Myrmidon Monk's mandibles sounds like a falling gavel. "Left's the only way to go. With our scout investigating ahead, of course."

"If I suddenly get whipped off somewhere," says Half-Elf Scout, "I hope you'll at least put up a tombstone for me."

You tell him that if he expects to get teleported away, maybe you should hold on to the loot.

"Oof!" He laughs.

"Yeah, nobody wants you giving us the slip," Female Warrior agrees. "Right?"

You say that you agree completely.

Female Bishop and your cousin look at you, still a bit disbelieving.

*We've come this far. If we can't trust our party members by now, what can we trust?*

It's the same way everyone has entrusted you with leading them in combat, even though a single wrong move on your part could get everybody killed. If the two of them are wrong and their suggestion wipes out the party, so be it. It's nothing to worry about.

So your scout leads, and you take a confident step after him down the hallway.

*Nothing happened.*

Hmm.

You sigh demonstratively, and then for the umpteenth time: *'Let's go.'*

You can hear the footsteps of the others behind you over the rattling of your own armor.

"What if he's not there?" Female Warrior asks tartly. "I mean... You know. What if we don't find him?"

"He practically invited us down here! I'd tell him to post some dang office hours!"

You glance behind you as you listen to Female Warrior and Half-Elf Scout chat. Myrmidon Monk is vigilantly watching everyone's back, while your cousin and Female Bishop look at each other and giggle.

*No problems at all.*

If you're going to die here, then your time to die has come. It's as simple as that.

Without reluctance, without hesitation, you kick down the first chamber door on the tenth level.

§

*Can't spend very long exploring this floor.*

A giant who exudes poison gas. Hordes of terrible vampires. A fire dragon, a frost giant.

As each monster blocks your path, you, and your party with you, take them down and advance farther into the dungeon.

Your blade sings, the spear thrusts, the knives glint, the spells are deployed, and you leave monster corpses in your wake.

Each time you get through a chamber, there's the dimensional warping again. You follow it to the next room.

Break in, fight, kill, and move on to the next thing. Break in, fight, kill, and move on to the next thing.

You hardly even know where you are anymore, but what you must do is obvious enough.

You and your party now move within the realms of the very greatest adventurers in the Four-Cornered World. If you cannot make it through this, then perhaps no one in the world can survive this dungeon.

There is only one possible thing that could stand in your way.

*Death itself.*

§

*Finally.*

You arrive before the door. For better or for worse, you arrive.

Standing before you is a thick door, just like all the other doors to all the other chambers you've entered thus far. As you stand and look up at it, though, you feel sure:

*Whatever happens, this is the end of the adventure.*

You take a breath in, then let it out. You look at the others. They all nod.

By now, you need no time to steel your resolve, there's no time to confirm with everyone. You only need to check your equipment and that of your companions and make sure everything is ready.

You've managed to conserve your HP, and you have spells remaining as well. Your equipment is in good order. No problems anywhere.

No pointing getting scared now: Even if you wanted to turn tail and run, you've been given no way home. If you turn around, all you'll find behind you are hallways that lead nowhere.

You murmur quietly, asking whether you and your companions should go. They reply that yes, they should. That's all; nothing more.

You give the door a powerful kick, knocking it down, and then your party piles into the room.

The dim chamber beyond is—much as you expected—just like all the others. Empty, desolate. Only wire frame, defining a stone square.

*This is the nexus of the Death?*

Frankly, the altar on the fourth floor would have seemed more appropriate than this.

There is, however, proof that you have indeed reached the inner-most room of the deepest level of the dungeon: a throne. An ornate chair is sitting at the far end of the chamber, and on it, a hunching, shadowy figure.

It seems to grow as it rises up, assuming human form and standing before you.

*The man in black.*

"Ha! Excellent work. Simply excellent." You hear slow, measured clapping. On the man's face, as the shadows fall away, you can see a smile of appreciation. It makes your skin crawl. "I had high hopes for you, it's true. But few are the adventurers who have made it this far."

"Dungeon Master…," says Female Bishop, in a voice that trembles for only a beat. "Who or what are you?!"

It's not really a question; it's a simple confirmation. Who is this person at the world's northernmost extremity, from which the Death spreads out over the land? This root of all evil? This greatest enemy?

Female Bishop, however, has a reason for asking—as does Female Warrior, with her oaken spear.

Anyone who has lost someone in these halls would have a reason.

"I don't care if you're an immortal wizard or the king of demons! What drove you to all of this?"

Female Warrior's question hangs in the air. Then the man in black laughs, a burbling sound.

He says only: "He's dead, you know."

The man shrugs. He sounds so calm.

©lack

Beside you, the tip of Female Warrior's spear trembles. "*What* did you say…?"

"I killed him. Or perhaps I should say, *we* killed him. It all works out to the same thing in the end. Ahhh, what fun that was."

The man in black rests a red-bladed sword, held in his right hand, on his shoulder and strokes his chin, speaking almost to himself. He sounds like he's recalling the taste of a pleasant meal from a few days earlier.

"I don't know who or what that was—so with many apologies I assure you, I can't answer your question."

The man in black almost sounds like he really feels guilty, as if to say, *So very sorry for defeating them before you got here.*

"If he's dead, why is there still dimensional warping around this dungeon?!" Female Bishop cries in disbelief. Even as she shakes with fear, she retreats not a step, her voice loud and clear. "We lost so many adventurers, and for what?"

"Please, please, don't misunderstand. I can't have you going around thinking I want to destroy the world or some silly business like that."

While Female Bishop and the man in black talk, you spare a glance at your comrades. Your cousin reacts first, sliding her short staff to one side, getting line of fire on him. The others follow.

Each of you moves slowly, ever so slowly, fanning out from the clump in which you entered the chamber to find your place. One gripping a short staff and focusing her awareness, one with a machete in one hand, the other forming a holy sigil. One with a spear, another with butterfly-shaped knives, each closing the distance.

You slide forward, too, inching ahead, judging the gap. You'll charge in and strike. One stroke.

"This is simply the *loveliest* place."

You're nowhere near close enough yet.

The man in black sounds like he's talking to a friend he bumped into on the roadside; he moves like he has all the time in the world, but his movements give nothing away. You watch as closely as you can, seeking any possible opening.

"Adventurers die, monsters die, and all of them come here, where they feed my power."

The Death.

*"What do you want? According to legend, the Platinum ranks are practically beyond human understanding."*

*"And now we've got this dungeon beneath our feet. What's down there? The Death."*

*"And if you delve into the depths and stand on the border between life and death, and come back to the surface... Then what?"*

*"Isn't it the Death coming back all over again?"*

The Death is power.

Adventurers kill monsters, monsters kill adventurers, and the cycle continues. The law of nature is being upset.

If that power, the Death, is in the hands of this man...

"All I did was put out a few treasure chests," the man says. "The adventurers did the rest—they went and died on their own."

"Don't get cute...!" Female Warrior spits at him.

"You wound me," the man in black says, then he chuckles and shrugs. "Everything depends on the roll of the dice cast by the gods. So why not do everything to stack the odds in your favor?"

"Gotta warn ya, Cap, it's no use listenin' to this guy. He don't make any sense," Half-Elf Scout insists.

"I don't care what he says," Myrmidon Monk clacks. "It's just the howling of an animal."

You take another tiny, sliding step.

You couldn't cut him before. What about now? Can you land a blow? No...

The red blade turns toward you, leisurely.

"It's of no consequence, really," the man in black says. "It comes down to nothing more than this: Kill and get stronger. Kill and be victorious." He's speaking to you. *Of* you. Yes, even you... "Even you enjoyed it, didn't you?"

*Strike him down.*

§

The light is faster than the sound: A red blade slices past your eyeballs, followed by a belated *whoosh*. One half of a dungeon tile. That's how narrowly you avoided death, just a shuffle of your feet.

You react immediately, closing in and bringing your katana up in a diagonal strike. There's a ringing of metal, and you feel a dull numbness in your hands. The sword bounces back. You were too slow, frustratingly slow.

Grasping the hilt, you sling your beloved weapon over your shoulder. No follow-up attack comes.

You see just the ghost of a smile in the dim light. It's laughing at you. Well, let it laugh.

"Hey, you, over here…!"

A spear comes stabbing in from the side. The voice seems so soft for one with a weapon so sharp. It's a female warrior. The two of you no longer need words to coordinate your actions. But that doesn't make you infallible.

"Hrrr-agh?!"

Another red flash slices through the darkness, and again the sound comes late, a clash of steel. Sparks fly, and the spear is deflected. Now the red blade describes a great upward arc. A strike from above. Her face tenses, anticipating the blow. But then—

"Whoa—!"

*Parried.*

A half-elf scout, holding a butterfly-shaped dagger in a reverse grip, just manages to push the blade off its path. Female Warrior smiles at him as best she can, in acknowledgment of his fine, light-footed entrance. Spear in hand, she struggles to get back to her feet. "Sorry, that one's on me."

"All good, but…I can't handle this one alone!"

With each flash of red light, Half-Elf Scout's body sports fresh wounds. He's a scout, after all. One-on-one combat isn't his calling. *I could use a little help here*, he seems to be saying.

When you ask if she can stand, Female Warrior says, "I'll try." Good.

You advance once more, your sword still across your shoulder, charging straight ahead and swinging three times. But the red blade blocks each cut, sweeping your attacks aside and always moving ever backward as smoothly as if it were melting away. Then suddenly, you feel a chill down your spine and jump back. The blade flashes through the space where your neck had been an instant before.

*That would have been a critical hit!*

"This sucks—it's six-on-one, and we can barely hold on! It don't make any sense!"

You agree with Half-Elf Scout. You would certainly like to settle this if you could.

There's an exclamation from behind you: "It's worse than that—look!" Myrmidon Monk sounds unusually agitated. It doesn't take you long to figure out why. Something is bubbling up from the darkness—or rather, somethings.

"GHOOOOOOOOOOULLLLL!!"

"GGGGGGGOOOULL....!"

Red eyes, pale, dead flesh grotesquely swollen. Dressed in rags and flashing fanged mouths, they must be vampires. Nightwalkers, nightwalkers, nightwalkers! And a great many of them, as if every adventurer to die in these depths has been summoned back from the grave. You have no idea how many of them might wait in the dark of this unknowable expanse.

"So much for six-on-one. Think your numbers were a little off," Myrmidon Monk says, his antennae bobbing vigilantly. He clacks his mandibles together. "Though it makes no difference to our plan—to kill them all. We and they have that much in common, at least."

"Well, there goes complaining about how we can't win despite the advantage in numbers," Female Warrior says. "Now they've got the numbers, and they're some tough customers." *Not fair at all.*

Your face is tight as you nod at Female Warrior, then ready your sword in a low stance. You slide forward, taking care to not lift your feet as you close the distance to your opponents, trying to find their presence. Where is the red blade? You can't make out even the silhouettes of your foes in the darkness. The idea of being able to sense an enemy's presence is a rather nebulous one anyway. Honestly, there probably is no such thing. There's only sound, the rasping of breath, traces of body heat, eddies in the air. The five senses tell all there is to tell.

Female Warrior looks at you, and you can feel the trust her eyes convey. She seems to have noticed how calm your breathing is.

"So," she says, "what's the plan?"

The edges of your lips curl up as you tell her that there is only ever one plan: Destroy each and every one of them.

*Heh.* She gives a good-natured shrug, her pale face breaking into a smile. It seems you've successfully relieved the tension.

"Mm." Myrmidon Monk grunts thoughtfully. "Would you like me to switch to the front row? I don't mind either way."

"Get outta town!" Half-Elf Scout says, despite the cold sweat drenching him. "Only one of us can chop off that bastard's head, and it's gonna be me!"

"Excellent!" Myrmidon Monk laughs, clacking his mandibles approvingly at the scout's show of enthusiasm. At the same time, he works his knotty fingers, tracing a complicated sigil. The Seal of Return.

"There's a good chance these undead are weak to Dispel...!" The one who calls this out is the party's female wizard, your cousin, who's incidentally also charged with resource management. "Three moves after Dispel! Let's do it! Coordinate with me!"

"Right!" comes the eager voice of the bishop beside your cousin, holding the sword and scales. The light has long since gone out of her eyes, which are covered by a bandage, yet her gaze contains the utmost resolution. She was weak once, but now she is a seasoned adventurer.

Even as you marvel at the bishop's growth, you grunt your own acknowledgment of your cousin's instructions, tracing a sigil with your free hand.

*"O my god of the wind that comes and goes, send home these souls!"*

Opening gambit: Myrmidon Monk's Dispel fills the space with a fresh, violent wind.

*Ashes to ashes, dust to dust.* The rotting corpses are unable to withstand this purifying air, akin as it is to the Resurrection miracle that restores life. The legions of restless dead in this dungeon were not summoned by a curse, but before a high-level miracle, they succumb just the same.

As the nightwalkers crumble into dust, your cousin's voice sounds loudly: *"Ventus!* Wind!"

*"Lumen!* Light!" continues Female Bishop. She brandishes the sword and scales, intoning the words of the spell as if delivering a proclamation from her god.

The words of magic invoked by the two women overwrite the very logic of the world, refashioning it and producing immense power. The wind turns to a gale, and even your eyes can perceive the light condensing.

And finally, you, too, speak a word of true power, unleashing it all with the sigil formed by your hand.

'Libero! *Release!*'

A storm of wind.

Blinding light.

Roaring noise.

And heat.

The grave-dark room, having nearly become an alternate dimension, is flooded with piercing light. Those undead who escaped the effects of Dispel now scream as their flesh boils away. There is nothing in the world that can flee Fusion Blast.

"Captain—!"

"Oh crap…!"

At least, not if it is of *this* world.

You are lucky. In response to your friends' shouts, you dodge, rolling along the stone floor. The red blade flashes before you, and there is a spray of blood. The spray is accompanied by a whistling sound. Like a rain of crimson, it spills from the throat of Female Warrior, right in front of your eyes.

"Hhh—rrr…ahh?!" She presses her hands against her neck, her face bloodless, before she collapses to her knees. The red blade slides through the air again. Overhead in a grim repeat of last time. It's moments away from decapitating her.

"You—son of a—!" Half-Elf Scout shoves the blow aside. But the butterfly-shaped blade is smacked away, once, twice, and then his abdomen opens. "What the—? Hrrrgh—?!"

You can hear the blade bury itself deep in his bowels. Blood comes pouring from the scout's mouth. With your companions fallen before you, you grip your blade and rise to your feet. That was two of them.

"…!" Your cousin speaks quickly: "They need healing! You focus on the front row; I'll worry about the back!" You've always respected the way she keeps her cool in even the most extreme situations. And so, even as your companions desperately invoke healing miracles behind you, you slide forward. You can still feel the lingering heat of Fusion Blast on your skin as you jump, lashing out toward the red blade with your own.

Your hands feel little resistance in response. The ash, all that's left of the nightwalkers, wafts up from under your feet as you slide forward again, trying to control your distance. Your opponent has pulled back, laughing at you all the while. You can see the grin through the rising steam.

*This is bad.*

"You have to get back…!" Female Bishop's voice comes at almost the same moment you bring up your sword. You heard it, you're almost sure: a mocking voice forming the words of a spell.

"*Ventos…lumen…libero!* Wind and light, release!"

You don't have time for a single passing thought. You don't sense pain or agony so much as simply emptiness. Sound disappears, the world around you vanishes. You don't know whether you are standing or sitting.

In reality, you've simply been knocked on your side. You open your mouth, but the groan that comes out along with your exhalation of breath means nothing to anyone. Only one thing is sure—the weight of your katana in your hand. You lean on it as you rise unsteadily to your feet, wavering like a ghost.

The presence— *There.*

Your companions lie fallen in this chamber. Female Warrior in a heap like a ragdoll, Half-Elf Scout utterly motionless. Myrmidon Monk is slumped against one wall, your cousin kneeling beside him. Female Bishop lies prone on the ground—and then your eyes meet her sightless gaze.

"I…an…till…fight…," she manages, her voice shaking as she uses the sword and scales to stand, looking like she might collapse again at any moment. You feel the way she looks. Your chest armor hangs off you; you undo the ties and throw it away.

"A shame, a great shame. But I'm afraid your adventure ends here." The red blade is in front of you. The bastard is laughing. That armor won't do you any good now.

At last, you hold your sword straight and true before you, though it might be meaningless. The red blade is the symbol of death. You, and your cousin, all your companions, are going to die.

There will be no exceptions. Not one.

For no one can escape the Death.

*Very well.*

Does it mean anything meeting your end with your sword at the ready?

"...!"

Someone is calling you in a voice like a scream. You hear the rattle of the gods' dice rolling.

And then before you can answer the red blade comes running, and blood sprays.

§

A dark hut. The smell of medicinal herbs. The odor of a sick woman. A tiger laughs in your ear.

"You're a master." Her finger extends suddenly, pointing at you, then at the air beside you. "And so is your opponent. However!"

The tiger watches you with languid eyes.

"Your opponent holds the masterpiece weapon, you the piece of junk. Now what do you do?"

You answer.

The tiger smiles.

§

"Wh—wha?!"

The sword seems to jump back of its own accord.

You feel as if you looked back over everything in a single racing instant. Is this what it means for your life to flash before your eyes? You don't know. But you don't have to—your body knows.

Your life turns like a great wheel, propelling your body forward.

*A movement that avoids a critical hit.*

The clear *clang* of swords, the first sound of surprise the man in black has made, all go swirling past you. Everything seems hazy except the feeling of the blade in your hand.

Magic Missile. Draw, attack. Two swords. Leap. You use all the skills you can bring to bear, yet you have more left.

*Yeah. What's left...?*

You smile. At the same moment as the smile crosses your face, the tension leaves your shoulders. Your breath flows around your body. You ready the sword in your hand with ease. You take what you assume cannot be called a fighting stance; you simply lift the blade up with both hands. That's all.

*Here's the moment.*

You come in from the side with a thunderclap strike from above, then flip the blade around. One diagonal stroke, then again in the other direction. Strike with the grip. Swipe across into a *hassou* stance.

There's a flash of light, and then another. Each collision of the blades fills the room with blinding sparks.

"In—incredible..."

Is that Female Bishop who spoke just now? It doesn't matter; you aren't distracted by it.

At this moment, the man in black stands before you with his red blade.

He said he enjoys winning. Getting stronger.

You can't disagree with him.

Yet—is that all there is to it?

Surely not.

What you've enjoyed to this point is not killing enemies or being victorious.

There's a difference there, thin as a sheet of paper, but there—like the difference between death and life and ashes.

You've delved the dungeon, survived deadly battles with your friends, been overjoyed (or sometimes gravely disappointed) by the contents of treasure chests.

It is not only victory that you've met on your travels.

You were decapitated by a ninja, attacked by succubi, to say nothing of goblins and slimes.

With fear, with clamor, hesitation, confusion, and the occasional stopping short, you've walked ahead.

What is it that has brought you so much pleasure?

Adventure.

*You are an adventurer.*

You heard rumors of the notorious Dungeon of the Dead and came to the fortress city to brave its very depths. Now here you are, confronting the source of death. If this isn't thrilling, what is?

*It all rides on the dice.*

Yes, you see now, it's true.

Even the gods don't know which way a battle will go.

Even the gods can't intervene in your fight.

All that is with you are Fate and Chance.

No one else's will is involved; nothing to force you to do one thing or another.

This is the true blessing of the gods. Could there be anything more wonderful?

*If the dice are to roll, let them roll.*

*You are free.*

If that's true, then…

"Wh—wha?!"

With effortless ease, your blade flicks back off the red blade and turns around.

You need only match your sword strokes to the flashes of light that burst out of the darkness.

Is it really such a great thing, to attain victory by killing?

Is it really such a foolish thing to die in failure?

Nonsense, all of it.

No one can determine the value of your adventure.

Not the man in front of you.

Not the companions who have walked this path with you.

Therefore, you need only shout.

Therefore, you need only howl.

The value of this moment, this instant, this adventure you've chosen.

This adventure is *fun*.

If you make one wrong step, you'll die. But so what?

If it goes well, you will live. Nothing more and nothing less.

Well then, what is there to worry about?

His skill and yours, the fate of the world, your companions, all recede into emptiness.

The ancients say: "*Have you a thousand foes, it is victory simply to face them with the conviction that you will fell them all.*"

Your opponent is a master, and so are you. He has the master blade, and you a piece of junk.

No need to worry.

There was never anything to worry about.

Roll the dice, adventurer.

Whosoever you face, the outcome of the battle you have chosen is already decided.

If one is the heavens and six is the earth, well, the chances of rolling one or six are the same.

Even if your chances were one in a hundred, the chance of that one is as good as any of the other ninety-nine.

In which case, all possible results boil down to just two.

Win or lose.

In other words, it's fifty-fifty.

You no longer need to think. You need no intellect.

Once you have decided to do battle, you need simply act as you have determined.

Nothing influences your free will but you alone.

Nothing can stand in your way but you alone.

How you move, how you swing your blade, are all at your discretion.

Form, skill—and fortune.

Your will and body, free now of all things, are in perfect harmony.

Mind and action are one! Let all be in concord!

*What's useless?*

You laugh. Free, clear, heartfelt.

There are no more doubts.

There is only prayer.

Pray and play, adventurer.

Just as you've come this far, treading on ashes that continue to glow and smoke.

*Yes.* You know.

You've known since you turned the first page that led to this dungeon.

Everything is for this stroke of the blade, for this samurai's sword.

This is, in other words…

STEP
8

DAI KATANA

The Singing Death

A blank instant.

The utter silence of the chamber is rent by one single, echoing sound: a high-pitched singing of the blade.

The sword tip flies forth—the flash of the red blade, that is.

It carries with it broken, shattered space.

"Wha…?!"

His eyes follow it. Yours don't.

You simply flick your wrist, flipping it over, the blade howling in your hands.

You take one step in, allow your body to ride the pushback. Your arms flutter.

You cut upward.

"Hrrnngh…!"

*Too shallow.*

The blades brush each other—*shhf.*

The man in black jumps backward, the smallest trace of blood oozing from his chest plate.

The look on his face is one of—emotion. Shock, or horror, or anger.

Whichever you choose to take it as, you don't understand it. You don't even seek to understand it.

You simply laugh. You're laughing. This is wonderful!

So far into the fight—but you are still in danger.

You take a modest step in, make a probing strike. If the man in black had still had his wits about him, you would probably have tasted his blade.

*Oops. Took that step without really thinking.*

Even that thought brings a smile to your face.

"The...the otherworldly blade is broken...?"

The murmur comes in a shaking voice, disbelieving.

It's Female Bishop.

She had been crouching in a corner of the room, but now she looks at you with amazement.

Her hand stretches out as if in quest of salvation, beseeching, but it does not reach you.

You advance. Forward. Ever forward. On to the next thing. Proceeding to the next paragraphos. Pushing on and on.

Because you have faith she'll do the same.

You don't know if that faith reaches her or not.

Either way, Female Bishop drops her outstretched hand.

The slim fingers are wrapped firmly around the sword and scales.

She rises to her feet.

"Well! I might just have a little problem on my hands...," the man in black mutters to himself. You mutter back that you think it's fifty-fifty.

*What's going to show up? What is he going to do?*

You judge your distance, ever vigilant. You know that with his blade broken, your opponent's range won't be what it was.

The man in black looks at you—and then he smirks. "Very well. Maybe it's time I started taking this fight...seriously!"

In an instant, he begins to exude vastly more power.

Not killing intent. Not simple rage. Nothing like that.

The red-black shimmer emerging from the blade becomes something that is indeed otherworldly.

*No...*

It is death.

The death of all those who have met their end in this dungeon.

Monster, adventurer. That great pile of corpses whose deaths were swallowed up somewhere in the dungeon—this is where they went.

They boosted the man in black.

It is, truly, a shining darkness.

The red light wraps itself around the man, entwining itself with him, melting into him.

This is the true power, the special power, of the otherworldly blade.

The man in black's power increases.

You think you sense something eldritch behind him. A swirling black shape. It looks like a winged demon; it looks like a wizened old mage.

*Ahhh.*

It must be whatever fearsome thing made this dungeon, its death now fodder.

None know how or why it became the master of this Dungeon of the Dead.

But if they did, you suppose, it would hardly matter.

In this dungeon, be there ambition, be there monsters, be there a Dungeon Master, all are equal before the adventurer.

Even the man in front of you now: If you strike him down, he can be killed. Just as, if you are struck down, you will die.

"Time for turn two," says the man, his white teeth flashing in something like a snarl. "Try to enjoy it, eh?"

*'Already enjoying it.'*

Your answer mimics his question, but also mocks it, and you bring your katana into a fighting stance.

You reach out slightly with one hand, holding your sword hand back—almost like you're pulling the string of a bow.

So how will he come at you? What will happen?

His range has grown shorter, but you aren't impatient enough to rush in.

Seize the initiative, or let him make the first move? It's a bad plan to let an unknown opponent take the lead, but it's no better to dive headlong into danger.

*Shhf.* You slide a foot forward, your sandal hushing against the stone floor.

"O gods!"

The prayer is like lightning that splits the darkness.

"＿!!"

You move too fast for the naked eye. Faster than thought. Your body seems to act on its own.

The man in black's mouth is moving, he's mumbling, incanting—that's the moment.

The red light, the blade, stretches out. What was lost is restored, sharper than before.

The great black *stuff* emanating from the man flares up and attacks. You simply meet it.

"Kyyeeeeehhhh!"

There is a red torrent of death, akin to Fusion Blast.

The death entwining around the man's blade assumes the form of a red-black bird and surges forward.

The phoenix unleashed from the stroke flaps its wings of death, onward.

Its aim—is not you. It is Female Bishop, who voiced that great prayer this moment.

*The blade!*

You match its movements, stretching out, striking with the sword in your hand.

Only now do you realize the blade has a chip in it. A single notch square in the middle.

Probably taken in some exchange with the otherworldly blade earlier.

But.

*It will not bend, will not break. This is a good blade.*

Therefore.

Therefore you strike back against the encroaching death.

"Wha...?!"

You don't cut. Nor even simply deflect.

Instead, you do as you did with the ninja before, sending the red flash back, piercing the chamber.

The blade, which a moment earlier *became* before your eyes.

The most secret technique of turning back another's strike. Much like spell deflection, but also not. The lost third form. The realm of the ascended, the enlightened.

The technique the tiger granted the child for sheer amusement now turns back death.

"Gyah! Gaaah!"

Is it a scream of pain or a cry of attack?

The man in black makes this eerie sound as the conflagration of death scorches him; even as he burns, he raises the blade to strike again.

Each time he does so, the death-bearing flashes of red light fall upon you like rain.

And you beat them back.

With a shout of your own, you turn, you dance, like the elf hero of old.

One move. Another. A dance of attack and defense, where the slightest misstep will see you dead. Move after move. Ever forward.

And behind you:

Female Bishop howls.

§

"O gods!"

The sword and scales clatter as she thrusts them aloft, the room fills with a sound beyond the crash of swords. The bandage around her eyes, the blue ribbon tied at her chest: the proof of what her friends have entrusted her with. She touches each of these in turn, and then her holy sigil, her blind eyes upturned to heaven.

Her sight pierces through the ceiling of the chamber, through the many floors of the dungeon, upward, ever upward. She calls out to the holy table of the stars where sit the players.

"I have come this far as a pray-er!"

It doesn't matter if she's been raped by goblins.

It doesn't matter if her former friends left her alone at the tavern.

It doesn't matter if she spent her days an object of mirth and ridicule at the bar table.

It doesn't even matter if her friends were swallowed by the Death within the dungeon, turned to ash and lost.

She kept walking.

Why?

"I sought no reward! To be shown a path—that was enough!"

Yes.

She does not pray because she wants a miracle.

Nor because she wants to be rescued.

The players in heaven are always at the side of their Pray-er Characters.

When they win, and when they lose.

What more could an adventurer hope for than that?

"What could a girl defiled by goblins ever—?"

"That's precisely why!"

This time, this one time, Female Bishop states clearly her own hope and desire.

It will be affected by the dice of Fate and Chance, of course. Even the gods cannot alter that outcome.

You accept this. You celebrate it. It is a true blessing, you believe.

But even so—indeed, even because—

"At this moment, I demand you roll the dice with all your hearts! Or else"—she cries out at the gods—"I will never pray again!"

There is an explosion of light.

"Hnggaahhh…?!"

The man in black—the Dungeon Master, formerly a billowing and growing shadow— instinctively hides his face from the flash.

So do you. It's as bright as if the sun, as if a bolt of lightning, has crashed to earth. Not something you can look directly at. You throw up your arms to cover your eyes. Squinting against the brightness, you look at her.

*Flare.*

It must be. It's the only thing that could produce this overwhelming light, banishing the darkness of the dungeon and the shadows of this chamber.

Wreathed in the encompassing holy shine, Female Bishop appears as something greater, something overwhelming. To you, she seems so large that you have to look up at her, so grand that you feel an impulse to kneel before her.

Of course, it's a phantom. The small young woman is still standing there, no bigger than she always is. But you can still feel that presence around her, enshrouding her.

A woman in pure white vestments, proudly holding aloft the sword and scales—her eyes covered with a bandage.

The phantom of a great bishop indeed, the very likeness of the Supreme God.

This is the true and proper outcome of the adventure Female Bishop has walked.

The place she has arrived, or will arrive, when a small girl gets up scared, shaking—but nonetheless endures, stands, and presses forward.

She's come this far to confront a catastrophe that threatens the whole Four-Cornered World.

What sort of goddess would fail to answer the call of her devout believer, such that her light could penetrate even to the depths of the dark fortress?

At this moment, that very deity is here…!

"Impossible… She can't have the Call God miracle, can she?!"

"Yaaaah…!"

With a shout that's even more holy than it is adorable, the Supreme God—or rather, or also, Female Bishop—brings the sword and scales crashing down.

One single stroke. That's all it takes to make the shadow tremble.

Another blow. The shadow is sundered.

A third. The shadow surrounding the man in black writhes in agony.

This is the primeval light, the boisterous footsteps that call out to the break of day. This is itself the light of dawn.

"Begone from here, you miscreant!"

Female Bishop speaks with profound compassion—but no mercy.

In dispensing judgment, one wishes to take circumstances into account as much as possible, though in meting out punishment, personal feelings should in no way intervene.

When facing evil, however, justice is needed.

Not justice as dictated by the gods, but justice that people have deliberated upon, chosen, and taken for themselves.

This is the very wish that the Supreme God holds for people and has entrusted them with—Law and Order.

"Do you respect and value only what is strong?! Then you are nothing to me—"

*That's right.*

To her. To you. To all of you. To all things and people.

"—but a hindrance to our adventure!"

Flare illuminates the three thousand worlds with blinding light.

An explosion of brightness, as if the sun was shining on the surface, but summoned by the holy sword.

There is no sound, no sight. Only a pure breeze blowing.

"……Ah… Urgh…?"

A feeble voice sounds. You know exactly whose it is.

Blinking eyes blinded by the light, you call her name—not her number but her name.

Female Warrior heaves herself up from the ground, supporting herself with her oaken spear, rising slowly. She touches her neck where it should be slashed and looks at you, disbelieving.

"It…it healed…"

The wounds inflicted by a critical hit and Fusion Blast have simply disappeared.

You reflexively touch the scar on your own neck. There's still a mark—but that's all.

Like Female Warrior, you find that none of the wounds you sustained remain anywhere on your body.

"Ha! Ha-ha…! Now, this is somethin' else! I think I might just become a believer in your Supreme God!" Half-Elf Scout is practically jumping for joy. His butterfly-shaped knives sparkle in his hands.

"Faithless, you are," Myrmidon Monk says as he pulls himself to his feet. "I'm a Trade God myrmidon, and always will be.

*"O my god the roaming wind, turn back the currents of the air, overlook the fall of the dice."*

A murmured prayer, and indeed, this seems to be what has happened. You were in the direst straits. You yourself were the only one left who could fight at all. Your party was nearly extinguished.

*Now look at us.*

Everyone rises to their feet. Everyone lives.

"How—?" your cousin calls, then dissolves into a fit of coughing. Finally, she manages, "How's…the situation…?!"

*Take a gander.*

The enemy's strength has been much diminished. His minions, too. His weapon. His magic. Meanwhile you, your party, are fit and ready.

"Phew…," breathes Female Bishop, who borrowed, even if only for the merest instant, a weapon of absolute power from the Supreme God. "I've done…the best I can…" Her smile is as weak as her voice, thin and spent.

She brought a god down into her body. You can only imagine how much that must have shaved away at her own soul, but still she stands. She is standing, supported by the sword and scales on one side and your cousin on the other.

"I can…keep going!"

You respond in the affirmative, and then the party forms up.

Your cousin has her short staff in her hand, directing things on the back row, watching for any chance to cast a spell.

Myrmidon Monk holds his machete in a relaxed reverse grip, his jaws clacking, reading the wind so that you might have the protection of the Trade God.

Female Bishop, the Sword Maiden, leans on the sword and scales and steadies her breathing, her unseeing eyes surveying the battlefield.

Half-Elf Scout gives a slight smile, and with a knife in each hand he drops his hips and searches for any chance to strike.

Female Warrior looks at the partner beside her, and a smile like a flower blooms on her face; she twirls her spear and stands ready.

As for you, you face the enemy squarely, ready to lead your friends into battle. You thrust forward with your katana.

It's the same as always. Nothing different at all. No, not one thing.

You've delved the dungeon. You've entered a chamber. You'll kill the monster, take the loot, and go home.

"What's all this…?"

Before you, the man in black—no, the Dungeon Master—holds his broken sword and stares you down. He rests the shattered red blade on his shoulder, the remaining shadow closing around him, and then he gives another deep chuckle.

Whatever he is now, it's no longer human.

If a devil stands before you, then you'll kill a devil; if a god stands before you, then you'll kill a god. So long as you move forward.

It's not because you don't like him or because he's in your way—nothing like that.

It's simply to prove your own skill, to show your own achievement.

In that sense, it might be easy enough to pass this off as cleaning up someone who's become no more than a sheath for a dark and supernatural blade.

The man who stands before you, however—his eyes glitter. He can see no future but one in which he slices you all down.

It's clear that he's more than just a fool at the mercy of his weapon. This is someone who was drawn to the otherworldly blade, served it faithfully, and earned it as his eternal companion—a fearsome swordsman indeed.

*A warrior demon.*

In front of you is more than the wielder of an enchanted blade. He is a sword master—that is the only term for him. It is no longer his weapon that deals death, but he himself. Because he wishes to strike people down with his sword, the world will be destroyed. Such is what he is. Such is what he has become.

He knows only battle—only taking victory, only subduing the enemy, only killing the foe.

And yet you spot in his eyes a hue of hesitation.

"You almost sound like...like you think you can win!"

You answer clearly: no. What did he say? It sounded like nonsense to you.

You, all of you...

...*are adventuring!*

§

"Shaaaaa!"

The man in black who has become an enchanted sword master

unleashes more bolts from his red blade, enough to fill your vision, and each obviously containing instant death, or true power equivalent thereto.

You rush to meet them.

*Zwish.* You race along the flagstones of the chamber, right, then left, moving at will, striking out with your blade. You no longer quite feel the utter oneness that you did before, but still you are free.

*Swsh.* The man closes distance with you, moving like a shadow. He does, indeed, need to be nearer than before.

At that moment, something soft comes flying past and wraps itself around your blade. It carries the faint fragrance of beeswax.

"*Arma magna offero!* Gift magic to weapons!"

With your cousin's incantation, a pale bluish light of force glows around your blade. There's something you must do even before you take the time to be grateful.

*Give me strength! Give me strength! Give me strength!*

You twirl your blade in a circle, deflecting the red blade, parrying it, sliding along it, cutting back, driving forward.

In the darkness of a room that is no more than wire frame, red and blue perform a dizzying dance, sparks flying.

*Ha!* You laugh. The otherworldly blade, broken. Your own katana, missing a chip. And here they meet, master against master.

It's fifty-fifty, indeed. Your skill, your body, and the roll of the dice will determine what happens... No.

"Nice work, Captain!"

"You've got it!"

You drag your sword up, trusting strength alone, then pull backward, almost rolling, trying to gain some distance.

From the left and the right, two shadows race in. Three silver flashes.

Knives and a holy spear travel in great arcs as they meet the red blade head-on and bounce back.

"Hah! Haaah!"

*Too light.*

The otherworldly blade—still deadly sharp, though broken—or perhaps the man in black, repels the other two attacks easily.

But in that instant, that beat, you are able to catch your breath.

You take a breath in, let it out. You brush the wax that slickens your blade with the palm of your hand, stretching it, and then you start forward.

"Gah! He's tough stuff! I mean, we expected that, but still!"

"Yeah! He's got us beat, and it's six-on-one!"

Half-Elf Scout and Female Warrior cry out as you pass by. The enemy's magic blasts are holding them at bay. You stand before them, entrusted with the rest.

Right, left, up. The deadly spells come at you from every direction, but you repel them with swift strokes of your blade. You feel as if you're letting your body simply move as it wishes, as if your heart's impulses *are* your skill—or as if, perhaps, you're simply lucky.

Whatever. This is another one: another deadly assault you've survived. You've protected everyone, gotten closer still to the enemy.

Again and again, the red blade strikes, and you repel; each time it withdraws, you fill the space with your own weapon.

"Hey! What should I do?" You hear clacking mandibles. "Healing? Support? Don't care either way!"

"I'm thinking!" your cousin shouts back almost in a scream.

What you're more grateful for than anything at times like these is that you are not alone.

In the midst of the vicious sword fight, it's all you can do to focus on the opponent in front of you and the other frontliners to your sides. But you know there is someone in the back row keeping a vigilant eye on everything, assessing the situation and giving instructions.

*Ought to say a proper word of thanks to her before I die.*

Sorry for the trouble, cousin—she'll have to handle it.

Thus you call to her as you square off with your enemy; you hear her taking a breath and, faintly, biting her nails. That's all the attention you can spare for what's going on behind you. You know only what reaches your ears.

"Ah…"

That includes harsh exhalations, followed by Female Bishop whispering something. Your cousin listens, asks something in return—then raises her staff and shouts, "Heal her, support us—in other words, both!"

"You've got it!"

Myrmidon Monk's prayer to the Trade God becomes a pleasant breeze, blowing toward Female Bishop. The blessing probably doesn't do much to restore her enervated soul, but it can give her back some of her energy. The sword and scales ring out, alerting you that Female Bishop has gotten to her feet.

Your cousin shouts to you, "Let's do it again!"

You know exactly what she means—how could you not? You've spent longer with her than anyone.

*What can you do that the enemy cannot?*

There is something.

Yes, yes there is.

You shout back to her to do it. That tells the other two in the front row with you what's happening. They know you well enough to understand.

"Right-o, we're on it!"

"Yeah, sounds pretty good!"

"What in the blazes—?"

*He's* the only one who doesn't get it.

Then again, even you and your party hardly understand everything.

You don't need words. Your cousin has had an idea. You've chosen to go with it.

All that's left, then, is for everyone to help out. That's all there is.

And it's enough.

"—are you talking about?!"

You parry his strike with your sword. There's a *crack* as the blades come together, and you find yourselves locked in a stalemate, each pushing against the other. The man in black shoves mightily, trying to cut clean through you. Your katana creaks—but it doesn't break, doesn't bend.

And therefore, you...

"Hrn?!"

...abruptly relax. The otherworldly blade that was pressing toward you whips upward as the man stumbles.

In that instant, you raise your sword with all the strength you can muster.

"Gnnggh!" The man groans and leaps backward, hoping for a moment to regain his lost footing. Of course.

If this were a one-on-one fight, that would be a safe move. But it isn't.

"…Heh-heh!"

Female Warrior's laughter, somehow simultaneously innocent and alluring, tickles your earlobe. She brings her lips to the tip of her holy oaken spear, gently, still smiling. Then she kicks the butt of the spear, twirling it once. It seems to dance in her hand.

"Watch close," she whispers, her voice like honey. "Here I…go!" You hear the *snap* of her sabbatons.

It's like the Valkyrie's own javelin; the spear becomes a beam of light racing through the darkness.

By the time he sees it, it's already too late. He can no more avoid it than he could a strike of lightning.

"Hrraaaaahh!"

The man in black, disbelieving, coughs up fresh blood, and only then does he register the spear that has pierced him through the belly. There's a *clang* as the spear strikes the wall, pinning the man against it.

"You…you bastards…! I'm not…done yet…!"

He claws at the shaft of the weapon with blood-slicked hands, trying to pull it out, but to no avail. The blessed oaken spear bears the grace of the Trade God. And here, a believer in that god stands.

*"O my god of the roaming wind—"*

A breeze starts up. It comes from nowhere, here in this deepest place in the dead space, and brushes your cheek. The pure wind blows away the shadows that lie over the chamber, dancing around the two young women, Female Bishop and your cousin. They hold hands like sisters, standing there.

*"—carry our hearts there and their hearts here!"*

When Myrmidon Monk's blessing is complete, the Transfer Mental Power miracle occurs. The young women, exhausted from using so much magic themselves, are revitalized by the support of Myrmidon Monk's non-human heart.

A short staff is held up, the sword and scales are raised aloft. Three words of true power, intoned together in the service of one spell.

*"Ventus!"*

Wind!

*"Lumen!"*

Light!

*""Libero!""*

Release our prayer!

The two voices overlap with one another, filling the room along with the light and the wind.

The result is an overwhelming, destructive heat, unleashed directly…

…at *you*.

You catch the blue-white fireball with your blade. It takes the heat into it, a spark burning.

The explosive force envelops you, threatens to fling you backward. You let your feet slide, brace yourself against the flagstones.

You even out your breathing. Take the burning air into your lungs. Keep a firm grip on your katana. One more breath.

Suddenly, you think you can hear the sound of dice being rolled in the heavens.

The gods are holding their breaths, leaning over the board; you can feel it.

At this moment, *this* is the center of the Four-Cornered World.

*'Eeeeyyyyaaaaaahhh!!'*

You howl as your nameless blade traces a silver arc, slicing through the chamber.

A ball of energy, neither phoenix nor dragon, tears through the dungeon in the blink of an eye.

The man in black brings up his broken blade to ward it away, but it's a useless gesture. As you know.

*This man cannot cut magic.*

"Hrrraaahhh?!"

The man reels backward, spraying blood as black as ink.

You feel something as you cut. Not just the bones and flesh of the man—the Dungeon Master. You slice through the shadow that lurks behind him.

It is the feeling of death under your blade.

A trace of heart, however, still remains in him.

You lock eyes with the man. Even soaked in gruesome gore, his eyes

still shine, still burn. He glares at you. His mouth opens, twisting in a leer; his lips move to pronounce some curse upon you…

"*Gotcha!*"

Half-Elf Scout darts in like a shadow and sends the man's head flying.

Not with his butterfly-shaped knives. Instead, it's a sharp strike with the side of his hand that does the deed. The head goes bouncing like a ball, *boink, boink.*

Even as the head rolls away, the awful grin on the man's face bespeaks the certainty of his own victory until the bitter end.

You let out the breath you were holding. Finally, you flick the blood from your blade and return it slowly to its scabbard. There's an audible *click* as it settles.

With that, the room returns to silence.

§

"Is…is it over?" Female Warrior whispers, almost unable to believe it, from where she crouches.

That whisper is enough to bring you back to yourself. You look around at the others, all of you standing there in the chamber. Everyone is on the brink of exhaustion. The gods' miracles have healed the party's wounds, but they've still survived a battle to the death.

You let out a breath. Your legs want to give out, but you force yourself to stay standing. You're the leader. If you must collapse, you have to do it *after* everyone else.

"Probably…I think," Half-Elf Scout says, almost under his breath. "I was so totally focused, I'm not actually sure." He moves languidly, with none of his usual quickness, approaching the body of the man in black. The scout was pouring all his attention into the brutal battle. No wonder he doesn't look as sharp or dexterous as usual.

Half-Elf Scout grabs the oaken spear, still sticking out of the man's corpse, and somehow manages to wrench it free. "Here ya go, Sis," he says.

"Mm… Thanks." Female Warrior takes the proffered spear and, still sitting, hugs it. You leave her to herself and turn toward Female

Bishop. She's the one who worries you more than anyone in terms of having spent herself.

She brought the Supreme God into her very body.

The flare that had filled the chamber has long since faded, but you know you can't imagine the burden it must have laid on her. You call out to her, and she looks vacantly up at you from where she's sunk down in a corner of the room.

You ask whether she's all right, and in a voice like she's only half-awake she replies, "It still feels...floaty in here..." Her pale, slim fingers brush the blue ribbon at her slight chest, and she nods. "It's warm... Yes. I think...I think I'm all right."

You tell her that's good. Then you pat her on the shoulder and say she did a good job.

She appears to ponder your meaning for a second, but then she replies, "Thank you," and a smile like a flower's bud appears on her face. As exhausted as she is, it still somehow reminds you of the smile you once saw her smile at the temple.

You're sure that at that moment, her friends were there, too. You're not sure how you're sure, but you are.

"Words of true power take a fair amount of enduring," Myrmidon Monk clacks. He's judged his entry into the conversation perfectly. He seems the least tired of anyone in the party, but no doubt he's exhausted, too. He leans against the wall, arms folded; he taps his head with an antenna and mutters, "It feels like everything inside your head's been scrambled. I'm impressed the girl could take it."

"Since it's the words of the gods, it's a blessing... No different from a miracle. That's why," Female Bishop says. She smiles again and laughs.

The aptitude for magic, ultimately, must vary greatly with talent. The same way you feel that, no matter how deep your faith was, you personally would never be able to make requests directly of the gods. Your dalliance with magic, with the words of true power, has taught you that much.

*Cousin's got to be under a serious burden, herself.*

Speaking of her...

"..."

Well, she isn't speaking. She says not a word.

She's still biting her lip hard, her face pale, her staff at the ready.

It doesn't *feel* to her like it's done.

You feel the same way.

You only feel like you swung your sword wildly and raced ahead.

Even if it turns out this is it—you can hardly just come to a screeching halt.

You're about to say something, about to pat your cousin on the shoulder, when—

"It's not over…!" she exclaims.

*Thoom.* The dungeon shakes. Not the chamber, but the dungeon itself, thrashing as if it were a living thing.

"Eek…!"

The floor becomes like a bucking beast. Someone just screamed—Female Warrior?

You dive to cover her, positioning yourself on one knee in front of her. You look around, trying to figure out what's happened.

"The dimension, the space… It's shattering!" your cousin yells.

*What?*

There's a rumble in the earth, somewhere deep. As one cataclysmic crash follows another, you're amazed you can still hear your cousin's voice.

"If we don't get out of here right now," she says, "this place is going to swallow us all!"

"Get out? Great idea! Any plan for how to do that?" Half-Elf Scout shouts back, bracing himself against the shaking and looking in every direction. "I don't see an exit!"

"Isn't there any kind of passageway that man was using?" Myrmidon Monk asks.

"…I don't know!" Female Bishop responds with a shake of her head. Rubble is starting to fall from the ceiling, *clickety-clack*. She looks around, desperate. "There might have been, but it's broken, warped! Gone!"

What to do, then?

Female Warrior looks at you pleadingly. No plan occurs to you, but you don't want to say that. You squeeze her hand and force yourself to think as fast as you can.

Crossing dimensions. Warping. Transcending space. There's a way to do that, just one—

*The Gate spell.*

"Yeah… That's the only way." Your cousin sounds as despairing as she does determined.

Gate.

One of the lost, forbidden spells—there's no one left in the Four-Cornered World who knows how to use it. The last people to do so were mages who teleported around the world at their whim. They could chant this spell as easily as flicking through a hand of cards, planeswalking where they wished…or so you've heard.

The stories have made Gate one of the great ambitions of spell casters in the Four-Cornered World.

Perhaps the mage who created this labyrinth was one who could bend space to their will…

It isn't simply that the spell's words of true power aren't recorded anywhere, nor that the spell is advanced or difficult to cast. Once upon a time, a certain necromancer, in his arrogance, chanted this spell and disappeared, never to be seen again. He met the same end as the unfortunate souls who ran into Gate traps in ruins like this one— you saw them yourself on your way here.

You must know where you want to go, where you want to appear. Holding the coordinates in your head is profoundly difficult.

After all, people can hardly put into words exactly where they are at any given moment.

"Aw, tell me you've got a scroll or somethin'!" Half-Elf Scout shouts.

A scroll—that would be a different matter. A scroll written by one of those ancient mages would allow you to leap from *here* to *there* in an instant.

Your scout is yelling that if you have one of those, he'd appreciate if you'd use it, and fast.

Already, the wire frame in one corner of the room is crumbling away like dust. You don't want to think about what will happen if it reaches you.

"No…," your cousin says, and her expression is as taut as a bow-string that's about to snap. "But I can chant it."

You suspected this might be the case. On the way here, she was always the first to notice when space was warped. And you saw her reading desperately through one of her spell books when the demons appeared, looking for some kind of solution.

It shouldn't be that surprising if she's figured it out.

After all, the most accomplished magic user you know is—who else? None other than her.

"...Will you let me handle this?"

That's what makes it so funny when she turns to you and asks you this question in an unsteady voice. You're about to ask how she can even wonder at this late date—but when you think about it, you realize you never really told her.

So you laugh, and say that if she can't do it, no one can.

Your cousin blinks.

"Got to admit, I've never seen you defeated in a contest of luck," Myrmidon Monk comments, his mandibles clacking like he's chewing something over. He places a hand on your cousin's shoulder. "So I'm betting on you. I don't want to wind up in some gods-forsaken dimension somewhere."

Before your cousin can fully comprehend the meaning of what he's saying, there's a tug on her sleeve. "I trust you, too. With you, I'm sure we'll be okay," Female Bishop says, smiling at your dumbfounded cousin. She's made it back to where everyone else is, veritably crawling, supporting herself with the sword and scales.

Compared with her, Half-Elf Scout's movements look light and easy as he sidles up to the rest of you. "What other choice have I got? You pull this off, Sis, and I'm gonna worship *you* from now on!" Then he crosses his arms, winks, and even puffs out his chest importantly. "All right, let's do this before we chicken out!"

Gods above! How many times has his laid-back attitude saved you and your group? He does it, even though he might be the most frightened of all. You grin, and your scout grins back.

Yeah—doesn't matter either way.

"...At least if we end up somewhere we don't like, we'll be there together." Female Warrior grasps your hand and pulls herself to her feet. Among all the rumbling and roaring and shaking, the support she turns to is her oaken spear—and you. She grips your hand, leaning on you, supporting herself on you, and then she looks up at you and winks. "So I'm not scared."

*Well, there it is.*

So you summarize everyone's opinions, then shrug at your cousin. The rest is up to her. You're all counting on her. If you have anything to say to her, it's only that.

It's enough, though. Yes, if you have to add anything at all, it might be—

*Won't give you any grief even if you screw this up.*

That, and not much more.

Your cousin's eyes, which have been fixed on you, waver. Perhaps with anxiety or fear, or perhaps self-doubt. She blinks several times, and the look passes. What's left is only her usual answer, as full of self-confidence as ever:

"...Right!"

The wire frame of the chamber is almost completely gone. You stand in the middle of sheer darkness with only the floor beneath your feet to tell you where you are. But the six of you are the first, and last, people to defeat this Dungeon of the Dead. So whatever happens, you have nothing to fear. You need only hold your heads up high and adventure.

You all look at each other and nod. That's the signal.

Your cousin holds up her short staff, and then intones the three words of power at the top of her voice: *"Z! E! D!"*

§

Blue.

That's the first thing you register.

The next, that you're floating. Falling. A shock.

You go numb all over, as if your whole body has been struck, but you're embraced by something sticky.

*Sinking.*

It's cold; you can't breathe. Your surroundings are dim, and your body feels as heavy as lead.

You're being pulled steadily downward by whatever has a grip on you. You open your mouth and something rushes into it—it's enough to make you think you've been caught by a slime.

You struggle; someone grabs your arm, clings to it. It's Female Warrior. You clasp her hand back.

As you try to pull her up, suddenly your arm breaks through the membrane. All at once, you heave yourself up.

Immediately, your senses are almost overwhelmed by bright light, fresh air, a breeze.

*It's the surface.*

"Hkk... *koff!* Hrgh..." Female Warrior hacks furiously. You rub her back and look around. It wasn't a slime after all. It's water.

You seem to have fallen into water surrounded by stone walls.

*More importantly.*

What happened to everyone else? Are they safe?

"The—the heck...?!" yelps Half-Elf Scout.

"Shit! I can't swim!" says Myrmidon Monk.

"Eeek...?!"

There's a series of noisy splashes as, one by one, your friends burst through the water's surface, looking like soaked rats. They each cough or expel water from their lungs just like Female Warrior did, but none of them seem to be drowning.

At that moment, you hear a voice.

"Wh-where in the gods' names did *you* come from?!"

You look up, past the stone walls, to see an utterly baffled soldier looking back at you. Your eyes meet.

You ask where you are and receive the perplexed reply, "The moat."

The already lively situation becomes livelier. You presume it's people coming to gawk. They start peering into the moat—townspeople, like you could find anywhere. Among them, just for an instant, you think you spot the shadow of the informant girl in her cloak.

You're in the moat surrounding the fortress city...

"...My mistake!" exclaims a relentlessly cheerful, innocent voice. Your cousin finally surfaces, letting out a precious "pfwahh" as she gulps in a breath. "It turns out if you go up ten floors from the tenth floor, you wind up in midair!"

She sounds so...unbothered. There's only one thing you can possibly say.

*'Stupid* second *cousin!'*

"You promised you wouldn't give me a hard time!" she cries. "You're the worst!"

That finally prompts your laughter to overflow, and once it starts, you can't stop it. She looks at you in disbelief for a second, but then she starts giggling, too.

There's no way to stop it now. You six adventurers, floating drenched in the moat, look at each other and break into gales of laughter. Female Warrior wipes tears from her eyes; Female Bishop holds her hand to her mouth as her shoulders quake, and still she laughs.

Half-Elf Scout finds time amidst his guffaws to call to the onlookers for a rope, while Myrmidon Monk clacks his mandibles.

It hurts; it feels wonderful. Will you ever laugh harder than you're laughing now?

And the sky. It's bluer than blue and clear as far as the eye can see.

"Don't tell me that after all this time, you really believed I was the third son of a destitute noble."

Facing the young king of the entire nation, you manage to constrain yourself to a chuckle and a *you little so-and-so*—but only because of your highly cultivated self-control.

You've entered the donjon of the fortress city for the first time, and a sturdy, indeed nigh-impregnable building it is. It's a solid stone construct, ready for any battle—you would never imagine it had been built in the tremendous rush to repel the upwelling Death.

Said to have been built by dwarves, today it is gaily and lushly decorated. That tapestry adorning the wall—does it depict the time the avatar hero retrieved the Elder Scroll from the underworld? Or does it show those who delved the dungeon in hopes of rescuing the ashen wizard who had been trapped by the beast of Chaos?

You and your group stand on a red carpet that has been rolled out for you, looking around nervously. You managed to dress up—somehow—but your outfit is still just a scraped-together mélange of stuff you found in the dungeon.

There's no way to hide that you are adventurers.

Granted, Female Bishop naturally looks like she belongs here, while your cousin and Myrmidon Monk seem unworried. But as for you, Female Warrior, and Half-Elf Scout—you almost couldn't say what expression is on your faces, not least because you're standing in front of someone who—despite the fact that you know him quite well—is the newly ascended king!

To cut right to the chase, the diamond knight sealed up the vile hole in the royal capital and brought peace to the city. The former king fell—lamentably, he succumbed to the evil that welled forth from the hole and died.

Such is the way of things.

As for the Vampire Lord who served the Dungeon Master, he was struck down by the Knight of Diamonds.

That's well and good. There are some adventures that needn't be any grander than they already are.

So then—it comes to you.

"Now, my adventurers, if you would be so kind."

As a fanfare announcing the completion of your duty blares, you and your group step forward and stand before the young monarch. In his hands is a small chest containing shimmering golden plates, which he raises reverently.

"I bestow upon you these Gold-rank tags." You all bow your heads, and he places the tags around your necks, the chains jingling. "Wear them with pride!"

You respond to him in the affirmative and strictly according to protocol (on which you were carefully briefed before the ceremony). Those assembled cheer and shout their approbation at your every move.

The six great heroes—the All Stars.

That is the nickname your party is given. You are the great adventurers who defeated the one lurking on the lowest level of the Dungeon of the Dead and saved the world.

That's not to say that anything about the six of you has changed dramatically as a result. Rank tags mean nothing in the fortress city. So what if you're Gold-ranked? Who will know what that means? And heroes? You're still you. Just adventurers.

If anything has changed, it's…

"What'm I gonna do with my fifty thousand gold…?" Half-Elf Scout muses with a sigh immediately after you leave the audience chamber. He's holding a leather sack emblazoned with the royal crest. It's as over-the-top as it is heavy.

And well it might be—it's packed with platinum coins. Even this formidable sum is merely a small portion of what you've been given, something modest enough to be handed over ceremonially by the king. When you think of the mountain of gold waiting for you in another room, it's enough to make you feel faint.

You can wade through the gold up to your waist—you could spend your whole life grinding for coin in the dungeon and never see so much.

"Let's start with a delicious meal!" says your cousin.

"I could never eat my way through all this. This is the sort of thing you invest—you know, put in the markets or into nice safe savings."

"*Safe* savings? Do you think the Trade God would approve of that…?" Female Bishop asks with a tilt of her head—but anyway, there's no rush to spend the entire sum. They said they'll keep it for you at the palace. (This seems to be a legend passed down from the time of the Platinum-ranked hero.)

You can take all the time you need to figure out what to do with it.

Suddenly, you avert your gaze. You thought you caught some sort of presence, a sense of something in the hallway Female Warrior is looking down.

A presence—is that all? You laugh quietly to yourself at realizing you can detect such things.

This presence takes the form of a small woman with silver hair. She's dressed in the outfit of a lady-in-waiting—which is obviously new, obviously stiff and uncomfortable, and obviously not what she's used to.

She trots up to Female Warrior. "Hey, you did it."

"Yeah…we did."

Their fists knock gently together, and they laugh like sisters. In fact…if they originally came from the same orphanage, perhaps they really *are* sisters; one older, one younger.

Female Warrior looks at the silver-haired lady-in-waiting's glue-stiffened outfit, then smiles like a cat. "That looks good on you," she says.

"No, but it's *going* to. I'll make sure. And that's enough," the young woman replies. Her cool expression never shifts except for a slight, sullen pursing of her lips. Dealing with the magical pit in the palace, then facing down the army of darkness, couldn't have been easy, however. If the six of you are heroes, the Knight of Diamonds and his party must surely be as well. Henceforth, he and his group will conduct politics in lieu of the palace's former advisers, who were all swept away in a stroke. You hear that at least one member of his group withdrew, claiming politics didn't suit them, but nonetheless...

*To quit and still be willing to stay on as a maid... That's not bad.*

"He'd be dead without me. Several times over. Pain in my ass."

So says the seventh adventurer in the diamond knight's party with a self-important shrug.

*Doesn't seem likely to get any better.*

Among the nobles in attendance at the ceremony, there were several whose faces were so studiously expressionless they might as well have been wearing masks. No doubt they were desperately trying to avoid showing the bile that must have been rising in their throats.

This imbecilic adventuring "pastime" had made a mess of everything.

For someone thinking only of what was convenient for them, it would have to be quite galling.

But it was still better than watching vigilantly for an ambush in the dungeon.

When you say as much, the silver-haired lady-in-waiting replies, "I guess," and nods.

"So you're going to be keeping an eye on him?" Female Warrior asks.

"That's my intention," the silver-haired woman responds, still unruffled. No doubt she hasn't forgiven that crack about her outfit, though. She gives a small, cold, yet soft smile as if she's spied an opening and says, "Best of luck to you, too."

What kind of face does Female Warrior make at that? You steal a look, and you can only describe it as uncouth.

§

"...So we hit pay dirt. That's really all there is to this, right?" Half-Elf Scout says.

Even with all the time you've spent in the fortress city, you've never seen it as lively as it is now.

Not because peace has prevailed or anything. There's a celebration, a festival to enjoy, and people are living it up. Among the crowd, you see some new adventurers as well.

Yes, there are still adventurers who come to the fortress city in pursuit of the Dungeon of the Dead.

There can be only one reason.

It has to do with your escape, which warped the dimensions deep within the dungeon, resulting in the discovery of the fifth through eighth floors, thought to be an ancient treasure store.

The man who caused the endless supply of loot using the power of death is no longer in this world. The ancient hoard is limited. Sooner or later, perhaps in the near future, the wealth will dry up, and the dungeon will be left barren.

Until then, however—at least for a little while—this city will remain a mecca for adventurers.

That impression only becomes starker as you approach the tavern. Meanwhile, you nod at your scout and say he's probably right. You now have more gold than the average adventurer will see in a lifetime. In terms of fame and renown, you can safely be said to have "made it."

"True that," Half-Elf Scout says with a serious look. Then he stops abruptly at the sign of the Golden Knight. "Hey, I've got a bit of business in here. You folks go on ahead, okay?"

The remaining five of you look at each other. You've never seen this expression on his face before. It's serious but not dire.

*Something we can help with?*

"Nah," he replies with a wave of his hand. "Gotta do it myself, or it won't mean nothing."

Very well, then. You tell him you understand.

"In that case," Female Bishop says with a nod, "I'm going to go pay my respects at the temple."

"Me too," Female Warrior adds. She's still hugging her spear, which she refuses to let out of her sight, but she smiles. "I've got to tell my sister how it went." Her smile contains no trace of the darkness or sadness it used to hold. To you, it is a joyous thing to see.

"Hmm, I think I'd like to wander around town a little more. You don't get a chance like this very often!" your cousin says.

"Maybe I'll join you, then," clacks Myrmidon Monk. You're very grateful—it would make you a little anxious to know your cousin was walking around out there all by herself. "What about you? Coming with us?" Myrmidon Monk asks.

You murmur something about whether it matters either way to him, and he clacks his mandibles noisily.

Then you say, since you have this moment, there's somewhere you need to go. Several places, in fact.

Thus you decide to split up here, and no one has any objections. With a few "See you later"s, you go your separate ways.

You're the last one standing there except for Half-Elf Scout, who glances at you and nods. "If this doesn't work out, I'm gonna come cry on your shoulder, a'right?" he tells you.

You say you'll let him; he grins, and with a "Bye," disappears into the tavern. You watch him go—and then you heave a sigh.

Before moving on to your next destination, you spend a moment watching the Golden Knight and the adventurers as they come and go. You and your party were here every morning and every evening. The stables and economy room were literally where you laid your head, but...

*As for where we rested...*

It was here.

This is where you consulted, chatted, ate your meals, laughed together, and let the tension drain out when you came home.

Now, though, you probably won't visit again.

Suddenly you hear a voice: "I'm looking for my older sister."

You turn around. There's a boy, tall for his age, walking down the main street with his friends. You see girls about the same age as him, and a tall scout in a black cloak—you suspect they're adventurers.

"I see. If she came to the fortress city, it's a safe bet she was looking to become an adventurer."

"That's right. The orphanage never had much respect for the likes of magic anyway."

"Sounds like someone who might be able to make her name in the dungeon."

"That's true. And who knows if the world might be in danger again sometime…"

"Hey, why stand around and talk? There's time for a tipple before we get started!"

You gather that the young man at the group's heart is a wizard. You find yourself thinking of a pink-haired girl you saw once…

Still chatting, the group goes into the tavern; you see them find a table and call a waitress over to make their orders.

It's the table your party always sat at.

*Hope he finds his sister.*

You offer up this heartfelt wish, then turn and walk into the crowds thronging the city.

§

"Huh! Didn't think I'd be seein' you around here again."

The shop is as gloomy and dank as ever. The armorer stops pounding on his anvil and looks at you.

He adds caustically that this isn't the kind of shop a hero usually visits, provoking a shrug from you. He could at least take pride in the fact that it was his shop that prepared that hero's equipment.

"Things don't change overnight like that."

No, they don't. You laugh out loud at this rambling exchange. How's the economy? Dungeon looking stable? You talk as if you might go back down there tomorrow, but then the man laughs and shakes his head.

"Doesn't matter. There should be money here for me for a while yet. When the customers dry up, maybe I'll move out to the frontier or something."

*That right?*

Eventually, when the wealth of the fortress city withers away, everyone will leave to go to other places. The Golden Knight, this armor shop—all of it will be left behind. You try to imagine the fortress city becoming a ghost town, then stop. That's years from now. Not so easy to picture.

Even then, after it falls to ruin, you expect this city will still be a place of adventure. That much, you think, is certain. You tap the scabbard at your hip.

'*Want to buy a sword.*'

"What, yeh feck up the last one?"

*Mm.* You nod, then give him the gist of your battle in the dungeon's deepest depths. The proprietor crosses his arms and listens intently, then finally mumbles "Ahh, I see," and scrunches up his face. "Frankly, that's a pretty unbelievable tale—but I guess it wouldn't do you any good to lie about it." He points at the swords hanging on the shop wall with a thick finger. "Pick whichever one you like. Tell me what it's worth to you. You name the price."

You tell him you're grateful for that, and he replies brusquely, "Call it a good-bye present. What you've done has cost me the food on my table in the long run, so buy somethin' and get out."

Talk about raking you over the coals. You share another laugh with him, then glance toward the entrance of the cramped shop. There's something new there since your last visit—you don't know if the smith forged them himself or acquired them; several slim katanas, much like the one you wield.

You take one in hand, loosen it slightly from the scabbard to look at the blade, then grasp the hilt to see how it feels.

You do this with several of the swords, when suddenly a small figure enters the shop with an "Excuse me."

"You again, lass?" The shop owner sounds less than thrilled. He isn't the only one who recognizes the girl—so do you. She's of small build, black hair tied back. The sister of the royal guard.

When she sees you, she makes a noise that might be a "Whoa!" or an "Oh!" then fidgets and looks at the ground.

You scratch your cheek, suddenly self-conscious. Everyone calls you a hero now, but you don't really feel like one; it's awkward to meet a girl who actually looks up to you.

"I know you want a sword, girl, but I think it's a little soon for you yet."

"But—!" The girl glances at you, then continues much more quietly: "I want to start training as soon as I can and get strong."

*You want to get strong?*

At her words, your expression turns inscrutable.

To become strong. To take victory. There's certainly nothing wrong with that, and yet—

Maybe the smith knows what you're thinking and maybe he doesn't, but he rests his chin in his hands and says calmly to the girl, "Won't your big sister get mad at yeh?"

"Well… Well, let her. I don't care," the girl says, with all the conviction of the young, the untried, who know nothing of reality, only their dreams. "I want to be an amazing adventurer!"

You heave a sigh.

You don't know his history, that man who was bent only on victory. No one in this world does. Nothing is left of him.

And you? What about you?

You, who are so sure that you're different from him.

As the thought crosses your mind, you reach for the sword at your hip as if it's the most natural thing in the world and take it off. As gently as you can, you hold it out to the young woman.

"Wha…?"

She's confused. She looks up at you in surprise, then she looks at the sword and goggles. Slowly, she reaches out with both hands, respectfully, and takes the weapon from you, a sound of amazement escaping her at its weight, which causes her to lean to one side.

You chuckle, then crouch down, planting one knee on the shop floor so that you're eye to eye with the girl. She looks back at you, her eyes wide and round.

You tell her:

This is the sword that struck down the bringer of death and broke his blade.

*It is a good sword, one that will not break or bend.*

For that reason, *you* will always triumph.

"…Th-thank you!"

You don't know how much she really understands of what you said. But her face glows as she hugs the sword to her chest and smiles happily. You run your fingers through her black hair, then stand.

"Dammit, you're stealin' my customers."

The shopkeeper laughs. Then you laugh and shrug. You're going to buy a sword. He'll make enough preparing it for the girl, polishing it for her.

"I did say you could name your price."

Yes, that he did, you point out, and then you draw a sword out of a barrel. It's a nameless piece, just another blade. It seems best to you— you just need something to hang from your hip.

"The blade that broke the otherworldly sword, eh?" You put some gold on the counter and the shopkeeper casts a quick glance at the weapon the girl is holding.

She draws it from the scabbard with fear and trembling, and with awe: the weapon that you wielded. The girl stares at the modest chip in the blade as if at the mark of a true hero. Will that katana be at the heart of more stories in the future? Will the girl's name be sung in sagas?

You don't know, nor does the shopkeeper. It's too far in the future.

For now, though, the shopkeeper grins ever so slightly and says, "That'll be no ordinary story of adventure. It'll be a strange tale from the fortress city."

§

You proceed to wander around the city, finally arriving at the temple of the Trade God.

There's the tall, tall staircase. Above, as ever, looms the windmill, creaking as it turns.

The wind gusts, blowing over the heads of the adventurers mounting the stairs, whirling through town and all about.

It looks the same as it always has. You ascend, one step at a time, your footsteps firm as they carry you toward the temple. For some strange reason, it makes you think of all the times you walked through the dungeon.

On the first floor, you encountered goblins and slimes and the like.

On the second floor, you tangled with the newbie hunters.

On the third floor, you fought the fearsome ninjas, then walked the border between life and death and lived to tell the tale.

On the fourth floor, you had a little dungeon exploration contest and took victory over that other party.

On the ninth floor, you faced down demons from another dimension and destroyed them.

And then—the tenth floor.

You and your party have had many other adventures, as well: all of them, you're sure, because you came to this town and met these companions. So if the Trade God is the patron of meetings and partings…

"Finally made it, did we?"

The nun stands with her hands on her hips, looking down at you and obviously not pleased. *Yes*, you think, *it's all thanks to her.*

You reply by way of explanation—or excuse—that you've been going here and there, and then you follow her into the temple. It's not like you had an appointment. You just had this feeling that if you came to the temple, she would be waiting for you.

"Your friends all came by earlier. They've gone home already."

Maybe the nun had the same feeling. She guides you along without looking back, deep into a deserted part of the temple.

The city is still celebrating. There won't be too many people rushing in looking for healings or burials, not for now.

"Let me guess… You want to put a seal on the path to that awful altar on the fourth floor."

*Yeah.*

So that was the favor that Female Bishop was asking for. It is her friends' resting place, and anyway, you can't let evil things use that place for their own ends.

People who want to destroy the altar may still appear, and the seal will not protect against anything and everything. But it's better than nothing.

What is your adventure but an accumulation of such requests?

"So?" she asks, turning to you in the silence of the temple. "What do you want here?"

Her expression is cold, even sarcastic. There's a flash of something in her eyes, just a hint that disappears as quickly as it came.

You let out a slow breath, then tell her that it's nothing at all—you simply want to say thanks.

In an instant, that cold countenance melts into a blossoming smile. "You're going to give alms! Yes, of course, we welcome donations!"

*Mm.* You nod, toss a pouch of coins on the altar, and say:

*'Never did pay for that information.'*

"_____"

The nun freezes in place. Her sharp gaze pierces you; you endure and return it.

You can hear the temple windmill creaking overhead, the wind blowing.

"Ahhh…" After a very long moment, the nun lets out a deep sigh and removes her wimple, letting her silver hair down in a mess. "I really thought I was careful enough that you wouldn't notice. I can't stand the perceptive ones."

Her tone has none of its usual stuffiness; she's giving you a compliment, although she's doing it in her own inimitable way. In your mind's eye, you can see the teasing smile, half hidden by a cloak, and you venture a question.

*'Wonder which one was the real you.'*

"I would never disguise myself before my god."

Whatever you expected her to say, that wasn't it.

The nun snorts and looks at you with a touch of mockery. "I get my handouts, and I pass the information along when I find the right adventurer. That's my duty."

The gods—the gods in heaven—would never interfere with the free will of the Pray-ers in the Four-Cornered World. But those people need information to guide their actions and decisions, and there's plenty of information out there that no one could possibly just know. With the world in danger, one god or another must have felt it would be wrong not to communicate that information somehow. A very Trade God-esque calculation—flexible and open-minded.

"Still…" The nun shrugs. "I meant it when I trusted in you six. Maybe I got a little too involved. I'll know better next time." When

ack

she smiles, she looks like a girl her age. Then she bows deeply to you, sending ripples through her hair. "Thank you very much," she says. "For saving the world."

You respond that it was nothing. You only did what you wanted to do, what you needed to do.

"You'd be surprised how few people are capable of that," the nun says, and then she looks up. The light pouring through the chapel's stained glass window drenches her in a dizzying panoply of colors.

You had the blessing of the holy virgin of the Trade God. How, you realize now, could you have ever been defeated?

She makes an exasperated sound at that. "By the way," she adds. "For my *future* reference, when did you figure it out?"

*Mm.* You nod.

It was because her chest, when you saw it during the Resurrection rite, was so beautiful and left such an impression on you.

There's no way you could mistake it.

"_____"

The nun looks at you with absolute disbelief.

The next second, her pale white cheeks flush, and for the first time, you see her stumble with embarrassment.

"Why...why, you! Get out of here this instant! You apostate!"

You duck the censer that comes swinging at you, trailing ashes, and set off running. You burst out of the chapel, then out of the temple, then down the stairs. The sky is blue and the wind is blowing. Behind you, as you run, you can hear clear laughter.

"We'll meet again someday—and I'm going to charge you for the look!"

§

With that, everything you need to do in the fortress city is done.

You take your cargo, your sword at your hip, and go back the way you came, toward the great gate. On the way, you pass the royal guard, dressed in military uniform as usual this time. Seems she's going to stand watch before the dungeon again.

"Doesn't look like there's any getting away from here for me," she says, adding with a chuckle that she hopes it dries up before her little sister starts delving.

Will it? You wonder. You give a noncommittal laugh. Whatever else happens to that girl, you're sure she'll become an adventurer.

"Well, see you, my dear leader. I think you had a good party." She pats you on the shoulder, then points out, "They're already here."

When you passed through that gate, you were three, but now five people wait for you.

"Sheesh. What kept you?" Female Warrior asks, crossing her arms and pouting purposefully when she sees you.

You jog up with a word of apology—now that you think about it, this is the first time you've seen her in traveling clothes. She looks like she could be a village girl from anywhere—but this, you think, is how she looked before it all began, although the oaken spear in her hand betrays what she truly is.

"I was just about sick of waiting for you. Real nice, going off and having a party all by yourself."

"You tell him!" exclaims, naturally, Half-Elf Scout.

You're surprised to realize how much his joyous tone becomes him. In fact, it's more than that—why is it that he's seemed in the highest of spirits ever since you defeated the dungeon?

"Heh! Because I'm a married man now!" he says.

*Well!*

You don't try to hide your surprise.

"Right?" Female Bishop says, putting a hand to her cheek and smiling shyly. "I gather he was head over heels for one of the bar waitresses…"

"Ooh! That padfoot, you mean? What wonderful news!" your cousin chirps.

You say that explains it, genuinely happy for him. When you think back, you realize he was always gathering information for you, about the dungeon and otherwise. The waitress must've been one of his sources. You nod. This truly is a happy ending. It's very much like your half-elf friend to see his labor bear such fruit—even when she never gave him any fruit on the house.

"So does this mean you're retiring?" Myrmidon Monk asks, his antennae bobbing.

"Nah." Half-Elf Scout shakes his head. "She told me to come back with a little more coin, so it looks like it's more adventuring for me."

"Are you sure she's not just using you?" asks Female Warrior with a giggle and a catlike grin.

"Oof...!" groans Half-Elf Scout.

It's chatty and lively as always with all of you. The thought that this will continue makes you feel—well, grateful, but...

"I don't much care either way," says Myrmidon Monk, anticipating your question before you ask it. "I'm happy to go back home and spread the teachings—or stay here and learn a little more myself."

In that case. You pat your redoubtable companion on the shoulder and say it would be a great help to you if he would come along.

"No reason to refuse, as long as you keep things interesting."

"Me too...," Female Bishop says, clasping the blue ribbon at her chest. "I want to do more... Enough for all of us."

Her duty was to become the hero who would save the world. Now that she's done it, no fetters bind her further. Yet she wants to keep walking: And it's surely her choice, her will.

You accept her decision, and a smile floats over her face as she says, "Good, sir!" and nods.

That being settled, the real issue is your cousin, standing innocently nearby and watching. She gives you a little grin, as if to say *Your big sister would be more than happy*—but does she understand the position she's in? If *this* is a planeswalker, one of the most powerful magic workers in the Four-Cornered World—well, what is the world coming to?

"Say what you like, your big sister is still worried about you!"

*Darn* second *cousin.*

She giggles, playing with the short staff she carries. "Besides, I still hardly know anything about the Four-Cornered World. Gate can wait a good, long while, right?"

You don't think Gate is as simple a subject as that, but it's certainly a very in-character decision for your cousin. The wizards of the world who are so eager to jump outside the board—what would they think if they heard her? But it's exactly because of who they are that they aren't standing here, and your cousin is.

ack

You don't say that—although you think she gets the message just the same.

Yeesh. It's going to be a real pain, having your *second* cousin around…

You make a show of muttering to yourself, but as you look around, your eyes meet Female Warrior's, with their striking violet.

She brushes aside her hair, an elegant sweep of her hand, then looks at you and, as usual, purses her lips. "Don't make me say it."

You shake your head. You won't, because you feel like saying it yourself.

*'I want you to come with me.'*

Just that one sentence. Just those few words, and Female Warrior blinks, then her face breaks into a smile.

"I will!"

So six adventurers are gathered once more. You and your group amble slowly through the great gate, leaving the fortress city behind. The great vast Four-Cornered World spreads out before you. Confronted with it, you suddenly have a thought.

*Was that really worthy of being called a secret technique, in the end?*

You laugh and shake your head: no. The fact that you felt like it was just proves your immaturity. Many a warrior, amid the clamor of battle, has grabbed hold of a flash of insight that has pushed their skills to the next level.

In that case, what you did was no profound secret way of the sword.

It was just part of the path to get you there.

From here, you could head for the fiery mountain or the forest of doom—it doesn't matter. Now that your adventure in the Dungeon of the Dead is over, a plenitude of new ones awaits you.

This is just the first of the thirty-three fighting fantasies.

And only one of more than sixty—and counting—*livres dont vous êtes les héros*.

Farewell! May your heart pound for your next adventure!

With that sincere wish, I send these words to you:

*Now turn the page!*

©lack

# AFTERWORD

Hullo, Kumo Kagyu here!

Did you enjoy the final volume of *Dai Katana*?

I put my all into writing it, so I hope you had fun!

I've traveled very far from home...

Why am I having that thought, when I haven't even drunk Mr. Saturn's coffee?

Is it because I've reached my first final volume as an author?

Or could it be because the origins of this story go all the way back to 2014?

That's right—at first, *Dai Katana* was something I wrote on the web, just however I felt at the time. But then life happened, and I put the project on hold for five years. Now it's been reborn as a novel series, and after three years, it's reached its conclusion...

I've written in fits and starts over that time, writing a bit, then putting it on pause to work on other, more urgent books, then starting again... It's taken me eight years to get here. In that time, I somehow became an author.

I've traveled very far from home.

With all those experiences, the original story has changed in a variety of ways. Although to be fair, the original story was one where I decided on the twists simply by a roll of the dice. People died unexpectedly, they got unaccountably closely involved with slimes, or they were careless and were nearly killed. The dice guided me to plot developments I could never have imagined.

The place where I stopped was—you guessed it, the moment when Female Bishop appears before "you" with her former party. When I resumed writing, however, I realized that I was going to have to handle things alone from there on out. I fretted about what I would do— but even so, I tried to write the story I intended to write.

Maybe some of you out there preferred the story the way it was before it changed. If so, I hope you'll still enjoy this version, the same way you might enjoy a theatrical version and a special edition. Me, I loved the straightforward forest ending of the theatrical version, but then again, we get to see more of Boba Fett in the special edition, which is cause for celebration.

This is pretty much the same thing. I guess.

In this book, "you"—that is, *you*—are the main character and become the hero.

This is something I learned from *Sorcery!*, the books that really sealed my nerdy fate. The one I got my hands on was about a magical crown that would make the wearer a great king—except that it has been stolen by the Archmage.

The Archmage's hideout lies beyond a wilderness crawling with monsters; it's not somewhere the army can invade. Instead, they send an adventurer—you.

You cross hills afflicted by pirates, brave an eerie cityport, and defeat the Archmage's assassins, a team of giant snakes...

To my young self, these adventures were tremendously exciting— although it took me a long time to get my paws on Volume 2!

*Sorcery!* has other game books that take place in the same world (although there are plenty that don't, too). Those endless stories, those endless adventures, were a major part of what drew me onto this road less traveled.

*Sorcery!* was, for me, truly a bronze-covered book.

There's another work that forms a major "motif" in this book: *Wizardry*. In it, "I," a nameless adventurer and my party, work our way through a seemingly endless dungeon. What party members I gather and what adventures we have are all up to me. It's my own personal story, forged one step at a time as the ashes cling to my feet.

It's also the story of many different adventurers and each of their tales. Both of these were very interesting to me and lots of fun.

Another influence I can't neglect to mention: *Legend of Lodoss*.

You might be aware of another *Goblin Slayer* side story, called *Year One*. I called it that because, well, it was a story of the main character's past.

*Dai Katana*, meanwhile, is a story of the world's past. It answers the question of what happened in the battle with the Demon Lord. Therefore, I thought, it is to *Goblin Slayer* as *Legend* is to *Record of Lodoss War*.

I knew I had to do a story about the All Stars.

All these influences and elements combined to create *Dai Katana: The Singing Death*.

I've traveled very far from home...

I could never have made it this distance all alone.

There were all the people who have enjoyed and supported this work for the past eight years, starting with the web version.

The admins of the aggregator sites who thought this story was interesting enough to include.

Everyone at GA Bunko Editorial who helped get this story out into the world.

All the distribution, marketing, and salespeople, and all the others who were involved in that process.

lack, who drew fantastic illustrations.

Takashi Minakuchi and Shogo Aoki, for handling the manga version.

To all my friends who chatted with me, listened to me, and played games with me—thank you always.

To my five party members who have adventured with me for eight years now.

And finally, to "you."

You who have picked up this book, adventured, and saved the Four-Cornered World.

It's all thanks to you.

I mean it—thank you so much.

And congratulations.

I'm sure you'll continue adventuring even after the end of this story. Maybe via video games, or tabletop RPGs, or even game books.

Me, on the other hand? I'm going to become a duelist, or maybe a king. Then again, I might not have a lot of time for that stuff since I also have plenty I need to write. There are 50,000 different things that might happen—this, that, and the other thing; tales perhaps told, perhaps not.

I'm grateful for it. Although sometimes I feel like I'm drowning in it. But still, I'll try my best.

Maybe we'll meet each other somewhere during your adventure.

My sincere wish for you is that whatever that adventure is, it makes your heart pound.

If your heart races as you wander, I will be overjoyed.

See you again—sometime.

GOBLIN SLAYER

He does not let anyone roll the dice.

WATCH THE ANIME ON 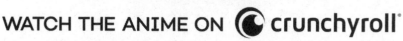 crunchyroll®